Sarah's
SONG

Sarah's
SONG

Wes Dodd

TATE PUBLISHING
AND ENTERPRISES, LLC

Published by Tate Publishing & Enterprises, LLC
127 E. Trade Center Terrace | Mustang, Oklahoma 73064 USA
1.888.361.9473 | www.tatepublishing.com

Tate Publishing is committed to excellence in the publishing industry. The company reflects the philosophy established by the founders, based on Psalm 68:11,
"The Lord gave the word and great was the company of those who published it."

Book design copyright © 2014 by Tate Publishing, LLC. All rights reserved.
Cover design by Ivan Charlem Igot
Interior design by Jomel Pepito

Published in the United States of America

ISBN: 978-1-63367-930-6
1. Fiction / Romance / General
2. Fiction / General
14.10.16

I dedicate this novel in loving memory of my mother,
Bernice Paulette Dodd.
Like in this story, music was an intricate part of Mama's
life. She had a natural-born talent, a gifted musician
and singer, which she shared with her family.
She also had a passion for reading. Unfortunately,
she went home to be with the Lord on February 17,
2014, three weeks before I could finish this story.
So, Mama, you now get to read it in Heaven. I did this
one for you! We will never stop loving or missing you!

Acknowledgments

Special thanks go out to my dear friend, Sandra K. Smith. Your time and help with this story is greatly appreciated. At the same time, your heartfelt words of kindness helped me through a difficult time in my life, the loss of my dear mother. Your compassion touched my heart, forming an everlasting bond.

1

A storm was brewing, not your typical squall, but a life-altering event was in the making. Spawned by a tropical hurricane off the east coast, giving way to its perfect alibi, this storm moved westward with direction and purpose, as if guided by some unknown force. Dark angry clouds rolled in, swallowing up the east side of Raleigh, North Carolina. Its unsuspecting victim, a prominent man driving a black Mercedes, was headed out of the city and into a path of destruction. Staring into the face of the storm, the man uncharacteristically continued into the path of darkness, as if driven by fate. The driver, a senior partner of a well-established law firm, was trying desperately to reach the safety of his home about a mile away, where his loving wife waited and worried.

Suddenly, violent winds lashed out at the man, sheets of rain and hail mixed with debris punished the Mercedes on all sides, reducing visibility to a bare minimum. Angry bolts of lightning rained from the sky like missiles from heaven. Angry gusts tossed the car about as if it was a play toy. The man was consumed with fear, apparent by the sweat on his brow and white knuckles clutched around the steering wheel. He began having flashbacks, not from his own childhood but beginning at the birth of his only child, a precious baby girl who was now in college. He was a devoted father, always making time for his child, especially for the milestones in her life. His thoughts drifted back in time, picturing her birth, her first steps, and first word—"*Dada.*"

In the blink of an eye he relived her entire lifespan, the good times as well as the bad, like when she lost her best friend in the whole wide world, her cat, Precious. The storm then relinquished one last blow, a decisive knock-out punch sending a gigantic pine crashing to the ground, crossing both lanes of the road the man was traveling. Knowing that his home wasn't far around the next bend, he thought he was within the safe confines of home. Unaware of the disaster ahead, he rounded the curve too fast for the low visibility. The man crashed into the body of the giant tree, just in sight of his home.

The dark angry clouds suddenly dissipated, moving out as quickly as it came, as if its job was complete, giving destiny the opportunity to alter a stable path in yet another unsuspecting young life.

✴✴✴

Meanwhile, one-hundred and ten miles west, in the city of Winston-Salem, North Carolina, a group of students from nearby Wake Forest University were participating in their Friday evening ritual. They were at Rock's Restaurant and Lounge where Friday night was karaoke night. Rock's was a place well known for its great food and spirits. Rock, the owner, a giant of a man with a heart equally as large, greeted everyone as if they were part of his family. Karaoke Night was very popular with the college crowd and locals alike. There were plenty who got up on stage as a joke or a dare knowing very well they couldn't carry a tune, not even if it was in a bucket. Then there were those who thought that they were really talented, the next big thing, all the while butchering some very good tunes.

Once in a blue moon comes that one in a million, a diamond in the rough, a person brimming with talent that everyone else can see except herself. Stepping up on stage was just such a person, Sarah McCray, the house favorite by far. Sarah was a third-year law student, determined to graduate at the top of her class. Friday night at Rock's was the only night of the week she would tear away from her studies, giving her brain a well-deserved break. Sarah didn't take her performances serious; even though she nailed every song she sang and received standing ovations from the crowd. She was focused on a career waiting for her when she graduated, a lawyer in her father's law firm back in Raleigh. This was something she had decided at a young age, the first time she saw her father perform in front of a jury.

Sarah approached the DJ for her song selection. The DJ nodded while gazing into her baby-blue eyes. Sarah, in painted-on blue jeans and a black and gold Demon Deacon T- shirt, stood on stage wearing that unforgettable smile of hers. Her honey-brown hair lay softly on her shoulders, blending in well with the gold trim of her shirt. She poised herself in front of the microphone as if preparing to give a performance at The Grand Ole Opry. The crowd knew her song selection the moment the music began. They poured out onto the small dance floor just in front the stage. Rock, who stood at the end of the bar, smiled wide at Sarah as he held up his tall glass of beer, signaling his approval of her selection.

"Strawberry Wine" by Deanna Carter was Sarah's selection. Everyone rose to dance, flooding the dance floor with dancers spilling out between the tables and chairs. Sarah took the microphone off the stand and walked slowly out to the edge of the stage, singing and smiling to her friends before her as if she was in concert. This was a song she knew well by heart, not needing to glance at the monitor for lyrics. She performed this song flawlessly once every Friday night, a favorite of her friends and one of Rock's as well.

Just as Sarah was into the last verse, her thigh began to tingle, letting her know that someone was calling. She overcame the distraction, finishing the song with style, a performance that would have pleased Deanna Carter herself. The crowd clapped and whistled as she descended from the stage. As Sarah was making her way to her table filled with friends and drinks, her phone vibrated, signaling a missed call. She picked up her apple martini and took a long sip. Before she could swallow, the crowd began to chant for more.

Danielle, Sarah's close friend whose hair was died jet black with bright red streaks within, took the apple martini from Sarah's hand. "What are you waiting for? Give them what they want." She rendered a devilish smile. "Give them some Shania."

Sarah grinned. "You really think so?"

Danielle snatched the solid black Stetson hat from her boyfriend's head, and then placed it on Sarah's head. "I know so. Go get 'em girl."

Sarah bounced back up on stage and was heading straight to the DJ when her phone danced a quick jig in her pocket, determined to get her attention. She shoved her hand into her front pocket, pulling out her sleek new iPhone. It was her mother who had called, which didn't alarm her in the least. Sarah and her mother were very close, more like sisters than mother and daughter. They spoke on the phone every day; even if it was briefly just to say I miss you and love you. Thinking nothing else of it, Sarah decided to call her mother after this song. She gave the DJ her selection then positioned herself at the microphone, her head tilted forward with the black hat pulled down, the brim shadowing her face.

The women erupted in cheers at the sound of the first note, piling quickly onto the tiny dance floor, leaving all the guys alone at their tables. Sarah's selection was one of Shania Twain's top hits "Man! I Feel Like a Woman." She hit every note perfectly as she danced with the microphone stand on stage. All the girls were dancing and singing right along with Sarah. When she got to the first chorus, Sarah whipped off the hat, slinging it like a Frisbee back to Danielle on the dance floor. Sarah's phone made another attempt to break her concentration but failed because she was putting on a show that would make Shania proud. Before the song was over several of Sarah's intoxicated friends had made their way up on stage with her, singing and dancing. As the song ended everyone including the guys was applauding.

As soon as Sarah stepped off the stage, a strange feeling came over her. Her iPhone in her pocket jiggled. This wasn't the same as a signal for a missed call or even a voice message waiting. This was a signal that a text had been sent. Sarah stopped in her tracks, obviously disturbed, by the expression on her face. She knew that the text was probably from her mother, which really troubled her. Her mother was old fashioned. She would talk your ear off on the phone, but texting was something she never ever did.

Danielle noticed the worry painted on Sarah's face. "What's wrong, Sarah?"

Sarah slid the iPhone out of her pocket. "I'm not sure. Mom's trying desperately to get in touch with me." She pulled up the text message. "Oh no!"

"What is it?"

Sarah slowly raised her eyes, her face flushed with shock. "Dad." She paused, tears filling her eyes. "He's in the hospital… ICU."

2

Sarah rushed out of Rock's, not taking time to say good bye to any of her friends, except Danielle. She called her mother while crossing the parking lot to her car. Her mother picked up on the first ring. "Sarah, where have you been?"

"Mom, how's Dad? What happened?"

"We had a bad storm," she answered in a shaky voice. "A tree was across the road." Choked up, she struggled with her words. "He must not have seen it."

Thinking only the worse, Sarah wiped tears from her eyes as she unlocked the car door. "Have the doctors told you anything?" The phone went silent as Sarah slid behind the wheel of her candy apple red Mustang. "Mom, are you there?"

"Yes, Honey. All the doctor said was that it was critical. Your father has a serious head injury. They're trying to keep the swelling down."

Sarah slipped the keys into the ignition and fired up the engine. "Mom, I have to pick up a few things and I'll be on my way. I'll be there in less than two hours."

"Don't break your neck getting here, Sweetheart. I don't need you in the hospital too."

"Okay, Mom, call me if anything changes. Love you, 'bye."

Sarah ran by her apartment, quickly picked up some bare essentials then poured herself back into her Mustang and headed straight towards the interstate. Heading east on I-40, she flirted with a moving violation as she weaved her way through the Friday evening traffic. Normally Sarah would set her cruise control dead on the speed limit then watch the idiots as they flew past, only to be pulled over down the road by flashing blue lights. Now the roles were reversed. It was Sarah, in a race against time, skating in and out of traffic, keeping a sharp eye out for the law. After skipping past most of the city traffic, where the cars were less bunched up, Sarah set her cruise, not on the speed limit but eleven miles an hour over, in hopes that she wouldn't run into a state trooper who hadn't met his quota.

With the car on cruise control and traffic thinning, Sarah's thoughts drifted to her father. She recollected all the important events in her life and how he was always there for her, something she had taken for granted. Up until now she had never imagined her life without him. Tears streamed down her cheeks, like raging water down a mountainside. Sarah wiped her tears away as she tried to alter her thoughts, concentrating on the road before her and the cars around her.

Drawn like a magnet, Sarah's thoughts kept drifting back, tears returning to her cheeks. She remembered, like it was yesterday, how proud her father was the day she got accepted to Wake Forest University, his Alma Mater. He surprised her the next day with a set of keys to a brand new Mustang. She also remembered how he took a whole week of vacation, using it to get her settled in on campus her first year. Sarah smiled, while wiping tears, as she recalled how he led her around campus, telling exaggerated accounts of the things he did when he attended. She had always felt that he was more excited than she was about being there, even though it was a life-long dream that came true for her.

Sarah's train of thought was broken by the ringing of her phone, which lay in the passenger seat. Figuring it was from her mother, Mary, and thinking only the worse, she quickly snatched it up. "Mom, what's wrong?"

"Nothing's changed. I was just checking on you."

Sarah released a sigh of relief. "Mom, you scared me. I thought something happened to Dad."

"No, Dear. He's still in surgery. Where are you?"

Sarah remembered just passing a road sign. "About twenty miles away…I'll be there soon. Is anyone there with you?"

"Just your father's partners, Jack and Michael."

"Did you call Uncle Billy?"

Mary hesitated. "Haven't gotten around to it yet."

"Mom," Sarah said, dragging out her name, "he should know. I know they aren't as close as brothers should be, but Billy should know."

"Of course, you're right, Honey. I'll call him right away."

"That's good. I'll be there shortly."

"We're on the second floor, in the surgical waiting room."

"Okay, Mom, love you, 'bye."

Sarah made her way to the hospital then quickly to the surgical waiting room. The moment she opened the waiting room doors, Mary rose to her feet, her eyes locked on Sarah. They both hurried into each other's arms as if they had been apart for ages. They were glued together, neither wanting to let go of the other, exchanging tears as they held one another. After a long while they walked hand-in-hand back toward where Sarah's father's associates were waiting. They had to step around two boys in the middle of the floor playing with Legos. The older of the two was a carrot-top with freckles. The parents were preoccupied with the third child, an adorable little girl with an overabundance of red curls. She was wearing a beautiful handmade dress, and she wanted everyone to see it.

Mary smiled at the little princess. "I can remember when you were that small."

Sarah blushed. "Oh, Mom."

"You turned heads everywhere we went."

Sarah pulled Mary closer. "The men were looking at you, and still do."

Jack McAllister approached with arms wide open. Sarah obliged him with a hug. Jack was the oldest partner in the firm. He was tall and lanky with thick snow-white hair and mustache to match. "Sarah, I'm glad to see you. I just wish it were under better circumstances."

"Thank you, Mr. McAllister. I appreciate you being here with Mom."

He pulled Sarah back, looking deep into her sad eyes. "It was my pleasure." His eyes narrowed. "What's with the mister? I've told you to call me Jack."

Sarah forced a smile. "Sorry, Jack."

The third partner, Michael Morrison, walked up placing a gentle hand on Sarah's shoulder. "Hello, Sarah."

"Thank you, Mr.—"

"My name is not mister either," he interrupted.

"Michael," she corrected herself, "thanks for being here with Mom."

Michael glanced up at Jack, then back at Sarah. "We are here for whatever you need. We're all family here."

Just then the swinging doors from the rear towards the operating room opened. A tall thin man wearing sweaty green scrubs glanced around the room. "John McCray family!"

Mary and Sarah went directly to him. "I'm his wife and this is his daughter."

"I'm the surgeon, Doctor Tillman. Your husband is alive. But by no means is he out of the woods yet." Looking up he noticed that every eye and ear in the room was upon him. He pointed to a small consultation room. "Let's speak in there."

Once inside, he motioned towards two empty chairs. "Please have a seat." He rolled a chair for himself, closer to theirs. "Mr. McCray is lucky to be alive. He sustained massive cranial damage."

"Will he live? Will there be any brain damage?" Sarah asked as she clamped to Mary's hand.

Doctor Tillman slowly leaned back in his seat, rubbing his chin with his left hand. "Brain damage," He paused. "We will have to run some tests to determine that. Right now our main focus is surviving the blunt trauma. The next twenty-four to forty-eight hours will determine his survival."

Sarah gave him a stern stare. "Your professional opinion."

"Like I said, the next day or two is critical." Doctor Tillman stopped himself, seeing that Sarah was not going for his runaround answer, reminiscent of a smooth talking politician. "Unless there is a miracle, there has to be some sort of brain damage. To what extent…that we will be able to tell in a few days."

A tear escaped and was rushing down Mary's cheek. "May we see him?"

"Of course you can. It will be a few minutes though. He's being transferred from the operating room back to ICU. At this point I think it is best if only immediate family sees him. I truly believe that the presence and touch of a loved one helps tremendously in the healing process. I can't show you where that is written in a text book anywhere…but from experience, I believe it to be true." He smiled while taking Mary's hand. "I'll keep in touch. Ask for me if you have any more questions. A nurse will be in here to get you once Mr. McCray is settled in."

The doctor left through the same swinging doors he came in. Mary and Sarah rejoined Jack and Michael. Mary told them of John's condition. They exchanged goodbyes, promising to return the next day. Sarah watched the two leave, then turned to Mary. "Did you call Uncle Billy?"

"Yes," Mary answered, a touch of reluctance in her voice. "He's in St. Louis. It will be sometime late tomorrow before he gets here. I'm supposed to keep him updated."

Sarah's eyes narrowed. "Why didn't he hop a plane? Dad is all the family he has left."

Mary shook her head. "You know your Uncle Billy. He does everything the hard way, or what is totally unexpected. He said that he and a friend would be driving in."

Sarah sneered. "I expect the friend will be doing all the driving while Billy does the drinking."

Just then the rear swinging doors opened once again, instantly drawing Sarah's and Mary's attention. A petite silver-haired nurse stood in the doorway. She peered over her wire-rimmed glasses, directly at Sarah and Mary, as if she knew exactly who she was looking for, then motioned for them to come. They followed quietly behind the nurse as she led them to the Intensive Care Unit. Once inside, all the nurses stopped what they were doing, their distraught eyes following Sarah and Mary as they passed.

The silver-haired nurse stopped at the room at the end of the hall. She turned, her eyes meeting Mary's. "Has Doctor Tillman explained Mr. McCray's injuries to you?"

Mary glanced quickly at Sarah then back to the nurse. "Yes. He talked to us briefly."

The nurse smiled, and then took both Mary and Sarah by the hand, her eyes revealing her sincere concern. "I just want the two of you to brace yourselves before you enter…and my prayers are with you and your family."

The two did not know what to think as they watched the nurse walk back up the hall. They turned to each other, grasping one another's hand, not knowing what to expect on the other side of the door. They entered slowly, stopping instantly, as if walking into a brick wall. They stood in astonishment. All the talking and explaining in the world could never have prepared them for the sight which now lay before their eyes.

3

Sarah clung for dear life to her father's hand the entire night, never leaving his side. The only hint of rest she received during the night was a few times she accidently dozed off, her head resting gently on her father's arm. It was the same with Mary, she, holding on to her husband, on the opposite side of the bed from Sarah. The nurses, like guardian angels, watched over Sarah and Mary, tending to their every need. For John, all they could do was watch the life support monitor while checking his vitals—his life being in God's hands.

The morning sun peeked through the blinds, warm rays landing softly on Sarah's face. Her eyes slowly opened, focusing on one thing only, her father, the one man she had adored her whole life. Nothing had changed. He was still barely clinging to life. His face was unrecognizable, swollen and bruised; his head bandaged up like a mummy. The only sign of life was the rising and falling of his chest with every breath.

Sarah rose slowly to her feet, her eyes turning to her mother sitting across the bed from her. Mary had also drifted off, overtaken by exhaustion. Sarah quietly stretched as she made her way to the window. She opened the blinds a bit, letting the warm sunbeams seep through, bathing her face. Slowly she shut her eyes, soaking up the sun, soothing her tired body from what seemed like the longest night of her life.

"What time is it?" Mary asked in a tired voice.

Sarah turned facing her, the warm sun massaging the back of her neck. "A little after seven."

"How long was I out?"

Sarah stepped to her father's side, her eyes glued to him. "I don't know. I drifted off myself." She paused. "Did you feel Dad move any at all last night?"

"I don't think so. He rested well last night."

Sarah turned her stare to Mary. "That's what worries me. Shouldn't there have been some kind of movement…a twitch or something?"

Mary stood, placing a comforting hand on Sarah's shoulder. "I know you're worried. I don't think he could have moved if he wanted to. I'm sure all those high-powered medications kept him out. It's probably for the best. I can't imagine the pain he'd be in right now if he came to."

Concern swept across Sarah's face. "I have a bad feeling. I can't help it, Mom."

Mary saw the distress in Sarah's eyes. "You always were the analyzer. You have never taken anything at face value. That's why you're going to make a great lawyer, like your father."

Sarah turned her stare back on her father. Mary, being the mother she is, could tell how Sarah was feeling, just by looking into her eyes, like reading a book. "Look at me, Darling."

Sarah met her stare. "What, Mom?"

"When was the last time you had anything to eat?"

Sarah slowly smiled, as if trying not to crack her face. "Yesterday."

Mary's eyes narrowed. "I figured that much."

Sarah's eyes fell on her father as she took his hand. "I'm okay, Mom. I'll be fine."

"Will you please go down the hall and grab a muffin and a cup of coffee."

Sarah glanced up at Mary, seeing that same look in her mother's eyes like she had many times before. It was the look that she wasn't taking no for an answer. "If that will make my mother happy."

Mary smiled. "Very happy."

Sarah stepped into the hallway; the aroma of fresh-brewed coffee filled the air. She followed her nose to the refreshment area located next to the nurse's station. An assortment of fruit and pastries were waiting by the coffee and juice machines. Sarah helped herself to a banana nut muffin and a big red juicy apple. She then poured herself a cup of coffee, the aroma arousing her taste buds.

Just as she was stirring in the sugar and cream, someone walked up behind her. "How are you holding up, Sugar?"

Sarah turned and fell into outstretched arms. "Uncle Billy."

He held her tight. "How's John?"

"He made it through the night."

"And how's Mary doing?"

"She's worried like I am." Sarah released her hold. "You flew in after all."

Billy removed his black cowboy hat, revealing an old scar over his right eye, and then ran a hand through his thick salt and pepper colored hair. "No, one of the guys drove me, but at times, it seemed as if we were flying."

Sarah looked past him. "What did you do with him?"

"He went to get a motel room to get some sleep. He drove straight through the night."

Sarah picked up her cup. "You want to fix you a cup?"

"I've already had my breakfast, Sugar…thanks."

Sarah locked eyes with Billy. "And I'll bet the liquid was brown, not black."

Billy grinned. "Guilty as charged."

Sarah and Billy talked while walking slowly by the nurse's desk in route to John's room. The nurses stared as they passed, checking out Billy in his tight jeans and cowboy boots. He was tall and ruggedly handsome, but the booze and cigarettes were taking a toll on his body, not to mention the lifestyle of a honkytonk country music singer. Billy owned his own band. They performed in a different city every weekend. The name of his band was The Billy the Kid Band, where country was the genre of choice.

Sarah stopped for a moment, staring at the door to her father's room.

Billy could see fear in her eyes. "Are you okay?"

She turned to him. "You had better brace yourself. He looks worse than you can ever imagine. He's lucky to be alive."

Sarah opened the door slowly. Mary was sitting in a chair by John's side, both of her hands clamped over his limp right hand. Her head was resting on her hands, as if she had been praying or quite possibly begging. She had her eyes shut, not noticing Sarah's and Billy's entrance.

Billy went straight to Mary, kneeling on one knee by her chair, his arm across her shoulders. "Hello, Darling."

She kissed him on his cheek. "Billy, I'm glad you made it." She looked into his eyes, hers filled with tears. "I'm scared, Billy. I'm really scared."

"John's a tough cookie. If anyone can pull through this, John can."

"Take a good look at your brother. Tell me what you see."

Billy slowly rose, then turned facing John, his only brother. He looked down at a face he did not recognize, swollen and bandaged. Billy and John were never as close as brothers should be. There was a five year difference in their ages. John was the baby, everything handed to him on a silver platter. Billy had to work and scrape for everything he had, and sometimes that wasn't enough in his father's eyes. John was always the innocent one. Billy still bore scars on his back for things that John did.

Billy left home on his eighteenth birthday to finally escape his father's iron fists. It wasn't until their father passed, a few years later, that Billy decided to return home. By then, there was an even greater gap in Billy and John's relationship, a scar that never healed. Even though Billy and John were never close, Billy still managed to come for a visit twice every year, at Christmas and on Sarah's birthday.

Time dragged, minutes passing like hours. It was well after noon and not even the first doctor had come in to check on John. Sarah had asked several nurses that morning, all with the same reply, the doctor is making his rounds. Along about 3 p.m. a teenage girl with pigtails and braces wearing a bright red and white candy-striped dress came bopping into the room with a beautiful arrangement of flowers in a vase. She placed them courteously on the window sill, and then asked politely if anyone needed anything. Sarah and Mary kindly declined. Billy had escaped for a smoke and probably a swig by the way his breath smelled after every return.

Sarah's eyes were drawn to the lovely bouquet. "Beautiful flowers…wonder who sent them."

"Probably the office," Mary responded as she rose. She reached over, taking the card out of the holder. "I was wrong. It's from a Jessie Beckman."

"Who is Jessie Beckman?"

"Wait a minute," Mary said, as she placed the card back onto the holder, "it's from Billy's band. It's signed from Jessie Beckman and the band…must be the one that drove Billy here."

Sarah rose, and then walked over to take a closer look. "That was sweet."

"What was sweet?" Billy asked as he walked through the door.

Sarah leaned over, absorbing their fragrance. "Who is Jessie Beckman?"

"Did he send these?" Billy asked while snatching the card.

"That's what the card says, from Jessie Beckman and the band." Mary said as she pulled a long-stemmed daisy out of the vase.

Billy and Sarah watched as Mary walked back over and took a seat by John. She took the daisy, placing it gently in John's limp hand. Her glassy eyes couldn't hold back her tears. "John planted me a whole bed of daisies one time. He knew how much I loved them."

Billy watched Sarah walk over and hug Mary around the neck, both teary-eyed. Sarah laid her hand on top of her father's, then clamped her eyes shut, squeezing out fresh tears. "Dad…please come back to us."

The door opened. A doctor of Asian origin walked in wearing a wide smile, as if it were glued to his face. "Good day. My name is Dr. Takahashi."

Billy greeted him with a firm handshake. "I'm Billy McCray, the brother." He turned to the ladies. "This is Mary, the wife, and Sarah, the daughter."

The doctor shook each of their hands. "Glad to meet you. I come check patient, Mr. John McCray."

Mary, Sarah, and Billy moved to one side of the room to give the doctor some space to perform his duties. The doctor patiently washed and dried his hands, then covered them with rubber gloves. He opened the chart and began reading out loud in a low voice, not English but in Japanese. He checked each monitor, jotting down notes as he went along. He took his stethoscope and checked John's heart and lungs, all the while making more notes. Then the doctor took out a small flashlight. He pried open the one eye that wasn't bandaged. Over and over he waved the beam across John's darkened eye. The doctor then stood silently over John for a long minute. He slowly returned the flashlight to his pocket, and then turned, painting on the same smile he wore when he came in.

Sarah boldly stepped forward. "Please Doctor. You have to tell us something."

"All his vitals look good—"

"The machine is doing that," she interrupted. "Is there any brain damage?"

The doctor broke eye contact, his eyes dropping to the chart in his hands. "Too early for that. He has long road to travel."

Sarah placed a hand on the doctor's arm, forcing eye contact. "When? When can you do the test? I know there is a test that will tell us."

The doctor pulled his eyes from Sarah, turning to Mary. "It is called a Confirmatory Test. It tests brain activity. We wait until he is more stable."

"When?" Sarah firmly repeated.

The doctor looked deep into Mary's watery eyes. "Your daughter is very persistent. That is good. I know this is very difficult on you and your family. Your husband needs to heal more. Seventy-two hours. If he doesn't regress, then we do test."

Mary forced a smile. "Thank you."

4

The next seventy-two hours brought about no change, for better or worse. Mary watched helplessly as her husband lay motionless on the bed. Little conversation went on between the three of them. Mary and Sarah would occasionally leave the room when a colleague or friend came by to visit. Billy would slip out from time to time like he had been doing; satisfying his two old habits that he couldn't kick.

Monday evening approached, closing in quickly on the seventy-two hour mark. Sarah knew very well what was in store come morning. It was either going to be a great day or the worst day of her life. She left the room to grab a bite to eat, not that she was hungry, but more to please her mother. Most of the people had left for the evening. About half a dozen people were sitting scattered around the dining hall.

Sarah made herself a salad, and then picked up a piece of irresistible apple pie, her favorite. While at the register paying, she noticed a young man entering. He was tall, neatly dressed in jeans, cowboy boots, and a red suede shirt. His dark bangs brushed the tops of his thick eyebrows. His hair on the sides came down smothering most of his ears. Sarah thought that he was cute, but the moment he noticed her stare she turned back to her food. Though she had an overwhelming urge to take a peek, she didn't dare look back in his direction. Her thoughts drifted back to her father, driving the attractive young man right out of her mind. She sat in a daze, staring out into space, as she slowly chewed her food.

"Excuse me."

Startled, Sarah swallowed her food. "You talking to me?"

He smiled. "Yes. Are you Sarah?"

Sarah covered up her confused thoughts with a smile. "Do I know you?"

"Not yet. My name is Jessie Beckman."

Sarah was suddenly concerned about her appearance, knowing that she hadn't fixed up her makeup or even brushed her hair. She began combing her hair with one hand. "You sent those beautiful flowers."

Jessie could tell Sarah hadn't spruced herself up, but it didn't matter to him. He was drawn by her natural beauty. "I'm glad you liked them. I hope your father pulls through."

"Thank you, that's sweet." She noticed his brown bag with a sub peeking out the end. "All the choices you have out there… and you chose to eat from in here."

He laughed. "Not exactly. I had to come refill Billy's flask." He threw a hand over his mouth. "Oops. That was supposed to be a secret."

Sarah smiled. "He has kept the flask hidden. But his drinking was never a secret."

They both laughed out loud.

"Anyway, I had better get back to my room. It was nice meeting you, Sarah."

"It was nice meeting you too, Jessie. You will have to come by to see Mom. She wants to thank you too."

"I will."

They exchanged smiles as they exchanged good-byes. For a brief moment Sarah felt alive once again. But as soon as Jessie disappeared through the door, so did that good feeling, the reality of her situation was taking control once again. It was a long restless night for Sarah and Mary. Billy was still with them but his flask had knocked him out for a few hours rest. At 9 a.m. sharp the door opened. In walked Dr. Takahashi and two other doctors they didn't recognize.

The oldest doctor, the one with a bald head and sporting a Duke Blue Devil tie, walked up to Mary. "Hello, I am Dr. Matheson. I'm the Chief of Staff. Will all of you please follow me?"

Dr. Matheson escorted them out of ICU and into a private consulting room. He sat behind a desk where there were three chairs waiting for them.

Sarah hadn't gotten her seat warm before she spoke up. "How long will this take?"

Dr. Matheson leaned back. "About an hour. We have to be thorough." His eyes then met Mary's. "I have a question that I have to ask. It is a routine question I have to ask everyone in your position."

Mary nodded.

"Does your husband have a Living Will?"

Mary shook her head. "No."

"Then you Mrs. McCray, being his wife, will have the authority to make any life-sustaining decisions for him."

Mary began breaking down.

Sarah grabbed her hand. "We understand."

Dr. Matheson ran a hand across his slick head. "I'm sorry...I had to ask."

Sarah glanced up at him. "How exactly does this test work?"

"We begin with the basics, brain stem reflexes...and of course the Apnea test to see if he can survive without life support. We also do a Cerebral Angiogram where dye is injected. Then there's the EEG and SSEP tests to check for brain activity and how electricity flows. It sounds simpler than it really is."

Billy raised a finger. "Are you ever wrong?"

Dr. Matheson gave Billy a sharp stare, answering first with his eyes. "No."

Billy rose from his chair and began to pace, in need of some medication of his own. "But there are stories about people who were legally dead, out for months. Then a miracle happens and they wake up."

"No, Mr. McCray. There are cases where the patients were in comas for a long period of time. There is a difference in being in a coma and being brain dead."

Billy stopped pacing. "Humans make mistakes, doctors included."

"That is true. That's why the test is done with two certified doctors. And if the test comes back negative, then the family may request another test with two different doctors."

"I'll be back," Billy said as he excused himself.

A few silent moments passed. Dr. Matheson rose out of his chair. "If there are no other questions, then I must leave to supervise the test."

Billy returned after a few minutes, odor of cigarette smoke lingered on his clothing. Unlike the rest of the time spent in the hospital, the next hour for the test flew by. It wasn't long before Dr. Matheson returned. The solemn stare painted on his face gave away the test results before he could speak.

Mary began shaking her head. "No, no, no."

"I'm so sorry," spilled from Dr. Matheson's lips as he sat down behind the desk. "All the tests came back negative. I'm here for any questions you may have."

Billy and Sarah both comforted Mary.

Sarah looked up at Dr. Matheson, tears running down her cheeks. "We want a second test conducted."

"I understand," he responded as he rose. "I'll gather up another team and begin immediately."

Billy stepped out of the room briefly, while Sarah and Mary clung to each other alone in the room. Sarah gently pulled back, looking deep into her mother's eyes. "Mom, no matter what they say, don't give up on Dad."

Mary wiped her eyes. "I would never do that."

Sarah took a tissue from a nearby box then wiped the tears from her mother's face. "I can find the best neurologist in the world for Dad. We can fly him or her here. Better yet, we can fly Dad there."

"I'd rather keep John close."

"Okay, Mom, if that's what you want, then we'll do it."

Billy walked in on the tail end of the conversation. "We'll do what?"

Sarah stood. "We are not taking Dad off life support. They can't make us."

"Okay," Billy responded as he took a seat. "Then what do we do?"

Sarah had a determined look in her eyes. "I am going to locate the best neurologist in the country...no, the world. Then we will fly him in to take care of Dad."

Billy studied that thought for a minute. "What if he comes up with the same conclusion?"

Sarah's eyes narrowed. She was about to pounce on Billy for his negativity when the door opened. Dr. Matheson entered with the same expression on his face as he did the last time he walked through that door. Sarah instantly glanced at her watch. One hour and ten minutes had passed, seeming like just a few.

Dr. Matheson sat down behind the desk. His eyes rose slowly, meeting Mary's. "I'm sorry, the results are the same."

Sarah stepped up to the desk. "We are not cutting off life support."

Dr. Matheson leaned to his right, looking around Sarah and into Mary's tear-stained eyes. "Mrs. McCray."

"My daughter speaks for me."

He leaned back, looking up, meeting Sarah's unwavering stare. "Do you realize how expensive this can be?"

"That's why time is of the essence. I need a list of the top five neurologists in the world. Can you supply me with this list or do I have to do some research?"

Dr. Matheson rose from his chair, a grin creeping across his face. "I can see right now that you are going to make one hell of a lawyer. I'll get that list for you. Give me about an hour. In the meantime, the nurse said that you have some visitors."

Billy headed out for a smoke while Mary and Sarah went to the waiting room. John's senior partners, Jack and Michael, were in the ICU waiting room. The four exchanged hugs, then all sat in a vacant corner.

Michael took Mary's hand. "How's John doing?"

Mary glanced at Sarah, then back at Michael. "About the same, no better or no worse. Sarah is in the process of locating a top rated neurologist. We want the best care for John."

Jack leaned back in his chair. "That's understandable, but this hospital is very highly rated. Can't they do anything more for John?"

"We don't think so," Sarah spoke up.

Jack ran a hand across his snow-white mustache. "What's their diagnosis? Does John need more surgery?"

Mary grasped Sarah's hand, their eyes locked. Mary nodded, giving her approval for Sarah to tell about John's test results. Sarah then looked at Michael and Jack. "The hospital has run some tests. They think Dad is brain-dead. We refuse to accept their findings. That's why I'm flying in the best neurologist I can find."

"Jack slowly leaned forward, shock splattered across his face. "Did you say brain-dead?"

"That's their conclusion."

"Based on what?"

"They called it a Confirmatory Test. Their results came back negative."

Jack shook his head slowly. "You have to get them to run the test again."

Mary noticed the strange look on Jack's face. "We did. It came out the same way."

Jack rose to his feet, his face pale as if he'd seen a ghost. "How did John know?" he mumbled out loud.

"How did John know what?" Mary asked, frightened by the look on his face.

Jack looked deep into her eyes. "The Advanced Directive."

Mary shook her head. Jack sat back down quickly, as if his legs gave way. "Mary, he didn't tell you, did he?"

"Tell me what?"

Jack leaned forward, his eyes glued to Mary's. "John had an advanced directive written up."

Mary had a look of disbelief on her face. "You must be mistaken. John may have mentioned it, but he wouldn't have made one without discussing it with me first."

"Mary, I signed it as a witness. I thought you knew about it."

Sarah could see that her mother was about to break down. "It doesn't matter. Mom has the power to make any life-sustaining decisions."

Jack turned to Sarah. "I'm afraid not. That document is legally binding and will hold up in any court of law." He could see Mary's tears rolling down her face. "I'm sorry, Mary. It's what John wanted. It's like he had a premonition or something."

"What do you mean?" Sarah asked, as she comforted her mother.

Jack ran a hand through his hair. "I've written plenty of these over the years. All of them were pretty much standard. But John's was very specific, as if he knew this was going to happen to him. It states specifically that in the case of brain death, he is to remain on life support only long enough to harvest his organs. It's like he knew ahead of time what was going to happen."

Mary's teary eyes rose to meet Jack's. "When did he do this?"

Jack hesitated. "Last week."

Sarah and Mary cried in each other's arms.

5

Sarah's attempt at changing the course of fate had failed. John McCray, by decree of his own advanced directive, was pronounced dead. Though death had reigned victorious, parts of John lived on through the harvesting of his organs, a caring gesture on his part. For Sarah, the loss of her father forged a permanent scar, a void in her life, like a black hole. She wasn't prepared for this, never imagining her life without him at this stage in her life. For so long she had been looking forward to her graduation day, first in her class no less, a feat making her father so proud. And then to go on to work side by side with him in a court of law, a dream now shattered, like broken glass.

Though Sarah's life was in disarray, she had to be strong, the crutch her mother could lean on in her time of need. Sarah reached deep within herself, unearthing an inner strength she never realized she had. She comforted her mother, while filling the position of head of the family. Billy was there for them both, though he wasn't much more than a stranger, due to the lack of family inner action throughout Sarah's life. Never the less, he stuck by their sides like glue. Jessie came by, paying his respects, before leaving to assist the band in their next gig. Billy was to stay on until after the funeral, and then a few days to spend with Mary and Sarah.

The church family, that John and Mary was so much a part of, stepped forward, tending to Mary's and Sarah's every need as far as food and house cleaning was concerned, like busy little bees taking care of the Queen. The loss of John McCray was felt in the church as well. He was an Acting Deacon, volunteering all of the spare time he could for the church and his community. Hundreds of people came to visit Mary and Sarah, paying their respects in many different ways. The visits seemed endless, draining Mary's and Sarah's energy by the end of each day. Billy tried to stay out of the way. Many visitors had to ask who Billy was, because he had become a stranger to this area. Only a few of John's oldest friends knew that Billy was John's brother.

Friday rolled in, accompanied by a cool fall breeze. It was time to lay John McCray's body to rest, letting the long healing process begin for Mary and Sarah. It was a perfect day for a funeral, if there ever was one. The Carolina sky was clear and pale blue. The leaves were just beginning to turn, with the maples surrendering first in a fiery blaze. The church, where John and Mary were members, was nestled in a group of maple trees. The bright white steeple of the church stood proudly above the blaze-orange tree tops, the gold cross on top shimmering in the sunlight. The church, which easily seated several hundred, filled quickly. The younger men found themselves courteously giving up their seats to the women and elderly. By the time the family arrived, the church was full with another hundred huddled around the doorway. Due to the injuries to John's head, it was a closed-casket service. Mary had picked out a fine portrait of John, which sat on a pedestal in front of the casket, as a memorial. After several of John's friends spoke, the preacher presented a nice, but short eulogy portraying John as a pillar of the community.

Sarah suffered through the most miserable day of her life. Other than a few obvious tears, she held her screaming emotions inside while consoling her mother. Billy on the other hand was right there for Mary and Sarah, although he didn't show the first sign of any emotions. He sat through the service like a good little soldier, but it was obvious there were other thoughts racing through his mind. Sarah picked up on it, touching his arm with her hand ever so often to bring him back to life again. She thought it was the alcohol taking him away; however, his thoughts were soberly clear.

The day finally passed, along with the weekend. Billy headed out on Monday, destined for Memphis, Tennessee, the next stop for his band. Sarah decided to stay home another week, receiving her class assignments through email. This was just the beginning of Sarah's life changes. When she finally made it back to campus the following Monday, she buried herself into her studies, even more than she had before, her way of coping with her pain. Her only focuses in her life were her studies and her mother, whom she had lengthy conversations with every night. Sarah began leaving campus after her last class on Fridays, heading home every weekend to be with Mary. Never again did she go with her friends out to Rock's on karaoke night.

✱✱✱

Time marched on with Christmas knocking at the door. Billy's band was playing in Atlanta for two weekends straight. On Sunday he decided to pay Mary a visit. It was in the middle of the afternoon and Sarah had been upstairs cramming for a big exam. She didn't know that Billy had come in. Sarah decided to give her eyes a break and head to the kitchen for something to drink. As she was descending down the stairs, she heard voices spilling out from the den. Upon her approach she recognized Billy's voice. Sarah was shocked because Billy and Mary were obviously arguing, not part of either one's nature.

Sarah walked into the room where Mary and Billy were staring down each other, anger apparent on both their faces. "What seems to be the problem here?"

Mary was the first to break the stare, painting on a fake smile for Sarah. "Nothing important, Darling." She turned her stare back to Billy. "Billy doesn't agree with my choice of tombstones for John…Right, Billy?"

Billy began softening his stare because Sarah had entered. "Yes, Mary. You know what's best."

Sarah walked to her mother's side, her eyes fixed on Billy. "Billy, don't you think the tombstone should be Mom's decision. If you had an opinion you should've spoken up before now… don't you think."

Billy turned his eyes to Sarah, and then forced a smile. "You're right, Sugar. I really came by to see how the two of you were doing."

Sarah had a puzzled look on her face, trying to understand why Billy had gotten so angry over a tombstone for a brother that he didn't shed a tear for. "We are doing fine, taking it one day at a time." Sarah noticed Billy shying away from further eye contact with Mary. "Are you playing in town?"

"No, Sugar. We're playing in Atlanta." He glanced at his watch. "I had better be going now."

Billy headed out the front door, while Mary headed toward the kitchen. Sarah was still confused. "Mom."

"Yes, Dear."

"What's up with Billy? I've never seen him like this."

"Too much to drink I suppose," Mary responded while walking out the room.

That wasn't a good enough answer for Sarah. She decided to approach Billy again if she wasn't too late. She headed out the front door and onto the full front porch of their Folk Victorian style home. Sarah was just in time to see Billy's Grand Cherokee rounding the driveway. She caught a glimpse of Jessie behind the wheel. They made eye contact and shared a wave. Sarah watched as the brakes lights lit up, sliding to a halt. Jessie stepped out and ran her way, not taking time to shut the door.

Jessie approached, out of breath but not interfering with his great big smile. "Hello, Sarah."

Sarah smiled. "Hello, Jessie. It's good to see you again."

"I'm glad to see a smile on your face. How have you been doing?"

"Okay, I guess," Sarah replied as her eyes wandered toward the Cherokee. She noticed Billy through a window, turning up a bottle wrapped in a brown paper bag. "I'm a little worried about Billy though. Is he alright?"

Jessie threw an eye over his shoulder back at Billy. "Something is eating him up inside." He turned back facing her. "I don't know what it is. He won't talk about it. He's drinking more these days."

Sarah could see the concern in his eyes. "When did it start?"

Jessie hesitated, not wanting to say the word. "Since the funeral."

Sarah looked back at Billy. "Maybe that's his way of dealing with it. He didn't show any signs of emotion during the funeral."

"I don't know. In the six years I've known Billy...I've never seen him like this."

Just then, Billy opened his door and stepped out. "Hey, Jessie! Do you realize who you are flirting with?"

Sarah pointed at Billy. "You had better set yourself back down before I come over there and straighten you out!"

Billy laughed out loud as he returned to his seat.

"We do need to go. I was wondering if I could call you."

Sarah smiled. "I would really like that. Let me go get a pen and paper."

"Not necessary," Jessie quickly responded, while pulling a pen out of his pocket. "I have a pen." He then held out his left hand. "Just right it on the palm of my hand."

"Okay," Sarah said as she stepped closer, taking his hand. "You aren't going to lose this, are you?"

"Not as long as I have a hand."

Sarah smiled while turning his hand palm up. She began to write her phone number down. It was hard because she was distracted by the scent of his cologne. Jessie was distracted as well.

Her touch aroused him; the smell of her hair was like a bouquet of flowers. She finished writing down her number then turned to him, only inches apart, face-to-face. They could feel each other's breath. The attraction was obvious for them both.

Jessie gazed into her eyes. "I know you have school, so when is a good time to call?"

Sarah's eyes were locked to his. "During the week is too crazy. I'm home every weekend."

Jessie's face saddened. "And, I work every weekend."

"That's right," Sarah responded, as she thought for a moment. "What about on Sunday afternoon?"

"Perfect…2 p.m.," he said, as he took Sarah's hand, kissing the back of it as if she was a princess.

Sarah smiled. "Oh my, a real gentleman."

"Billy taught me everything there is to know about how to treat a lady."

The smile was still frozen to Sarah's face. "Oh he did, did he?"

Jessie smiled while walking away backwards. "That's right. I just haven't had a lady to practice it on."

They both exchanged smiles and waves as Jessie was leaving.

6

The next Sunday was the last one before the Christmas break, or winter break as they are now called. After church and a nice lunch with her mother, Sarah escaped to her room where she waited eagerly for Jessie's call. At 2 p.m., on the dot, Sarah's phone sprang to life with the ring tone of "Pontoon," a catchy tune belonging to Little Big Town. She didn't recognize the number on the Caller ID, but answered anyway, assuming it was Jessie. Her assumptions were correct. Jessie called like he had promised, just like a true gentleman. Sarah curled up on a mountain of pillows that were piled on her bed. She talked, with the phone in one hand, while the other was rubbing her cat, Grayson. After an hour of small talk, much to Grayson's delight, Sarah ended the call, falling backwards on her soft bed, a smile bonded to her face. Though this was their first conversation, Sarah sensed something special in the making. Jessie was having the exact same feelings.

The next weekend rolled around, and Sarah was home for winter break. It was Saturday morning, the day of the week that Mary usually slept in. For reasons beyond her control, Mary could not sleep late this morning. She tossed and turned for about an hour, then surrendered and rose out of bed. From the top of the stairs, Mary noticed music coming from her kitchen. She descended slowly down the stairs while listening to Sarah sing along with the music. She remembered Sarah singing in the youth choir as a teen, but this was much different. Mary listened as she quietly eased her way toward the kitchen. Sarah was standing over the sink, her back to Mary, singing "Jesus Take the Wheel," one of Mary's favorite songs by her favorite singer, Carrie Underwood.

Mary stood frozen in amazement that Sarah was singing in perfect rhythm with Carrie, both hitting the high notes fearlessly. She remained in the doorway unnoticed, while Sarah was performing a duo with Carrie; her hands up high as she sang the words in the chorus. The sound of Sarah's voice triggered a mountain of guilt that Mary had hidden deep down inside, guilt that she was hoping would never surface again. With every word Sarah sang, Mary's guilt began rising, like the tide in the ocean. As it rose, it brought forth a flood of emotions, tears flowing like a river.

Sarah noticed Mary out the corner of her eye. When she turned, Mary was standing in the doorway, drenched in tears. Sarah quickly turned the radio off then ran to Mary, wrapping her up with her arms. "I'm sorry, Mom. I thought you were asleep."

Sarah held Mary. "I shouldn't have been playing that song. I know it brings up thoughts of Dad."

Mary began shaking her head on Sarah's shoulder. Sarah slowly pulled her back, looking her in her eyes. Through the tears Sarah could see a strange look on her Mother's face, a look of guilt she had never seen before. "Mom, what is wrong with you?"

"I'll be all right after a cup of coffee."

Sarah helped Mary in a seat at the table. "Sit right here, Mom. I'll fix you a cup."

Mary took a napkin from the holder, and then began wiping her tears. Sarah filled a cup with coffee, and then brought it to the table. Mary blew into the cup then took a cautious sip of the hot coffee. Sarah watched her curiously as she took a second sip, her hands trembling when she lowered the cup to the table.

Sarah took Mary's hands. "Mom, you're trembling. What's the matter?"

"I'll be fine. I just need to relax for a minute." Mary slowly lifted her eyes, meeting Sarah's. "Where did you learn to sing like that?"

Sarah grinned. "What that? I guess I've been getting a lot of practice at the karaoke bar the last couple of years."

"I remember hearing you sing at church…but never like that. Sweetheart, you have talent."

Sarah laughed. "Oh, Mom, I was just having some fun."

"Sweetheart, I'm serious. You have something special." Mary took a close look at her daughter. After a moment, she knew what she must do. "Have you ever thought of pursuing a singing career?"

"And what then, Mom…be like Uncle Billy, playing in bars and night clubs every weekend? That's not the life I want to live! I will have a position waiting for me in the firm after I graduate. I can always sing for fun if I want."

"Have you ever thought about American Idol?"

Sarah stood up, taking Mary's cup to freshen it up. "You sound like my friends at school. They all wanted me to try out when they were doing auditions in Atlanta."

"See there, it's not just your mother that thinks you have talent. Your friends do, too. You should have gone! Why didn't you say something to me about it?"

Sarah set the fresh cup in front of Mary. "I toyed with the idea for a bit. However, it would've been too much time away from my studies. Anyway, it would've been a long shot. The one with the most talent doesn't always win. It's a popularity contest too."

Mary slowly lowered her eyes, looking into her cup of coffee with thoughts racing through her mind, driven by an overwhelming guilt. Though it was hard, she knew she must continue. "Where do you think you got your talent from?"

"Come on, Mom. Why do you keep calling it talent? Yes I can sing. But so can you. I remember you singing at church."

"Not the way I heard you singing just now."

"Then I guess it's a combination…from you and the McCray side of the family. Dad couldn't sing a lick, but Billy can."

"There is something about Billy you don't know." She took a sip of coffee, drawing Sarah's full attention. "Billy was adopted."

Sarah's eyes flew wide open. "Adopted? How come I never knew this?"

"It was something your grandfather wasn't proud of, especially after John was born."

"I don't understand. You adopt because you want a child."

"That's true. And they did at that time. Your grandfather had a low sperm count. It wasn't impossible for him to bear a child, but highly unlikely. After many years of trying, they decided to adopt. They went to Atlanta and brought back an infant…Billy. He came from an unwed mother. Your grandfather even gave him his own name…William. Then five years later a miracle happened… John. Your grandfather was angry at himself for giving his name to Billy, who wasn't his own blood. Over the years he took out his anger on Billy. Billy had it hard; whereas John was spoiled."

"Come on, Mom. Are you serious?"

"Yes, Billy got beatings for any and everything. On his eighteenth birthday, three months before he was to graduate, Billy was told that he was adopted. And I'm sure there was a lot more than that said. How do you like that for a birthday gift? Billy took off that day, didn't even graduate. He never returned, not until your grandfather had passed away."

"That explains why Billy and Dad were never close. Well, Mom, I guess I got my so called talent from you after all." Mary gently rose from her chair, her cup in hand and walked slowly toward the sink. Sarah's eyes were glued to Mary as she studied her mother's strange behavior. Mary stood silently at the sink, her two hands cradling her cup as she took another sip while her eyes were drawn to something through the small kitchen window. Her vision was locked, not in the present; it was locked on a memory from the past, a memory never forgotten, just tucked away for safe keeping.

"I can remember it like it was yesterday," Mary said as she held a constant stare through the window. "John and I had been considering adopting. We had been trying for years." She took a sip of coffee. "It was five years to be exact. It was our fifth wedding anniversary. It was a Friday. John had called saying he would be late. That wasn't unusual. John worked hard on all of his cases. He was trying to make a name for himself. He promised to take me out to dinner later that evening."

Mary polished off her cup of coffee, and then placed the cup in the sink. She turned, finally making eye contact with Sarah. "Me, being the good little wife, decided to surprise him. Instead of him driving home and then driving back into town for dinner, I thought I would meet him at the office." Mary's faced filled with anger. "I surprised him alright…with his new secretary!"

"Mom!"

"That's right. I stormed out of there before he could get his pants back on. I drove and drove, crying nonstop as the miles flew by. I'm surprised I didn't run out of gas. If it hadn't been for the warning light I would have. Luckily, I saw it and pulled off the interstate for gas. I was in Greensboro." Mary returned to her seat. "I heard music coming from across the road. It was a bar of some kind. That's when I decided to drink my pain away."

Sarah's mouth flew open. "I've never seen you drink."

"And this is the reason why. I went in and guess who was there?"

"Elvis."

"No silly, I'm not that old. It was your Uncle Billy. This was before he owned his own band. I can't even remember the name of the band. He spotted me when I came through the door. He left the stage in the middle of a song. I don't think his boss was happy with that. I told him what had happened. I also told him that I wasn't leaving until I drank enough to kill the pain."

"That is hard for me to picture."

"Well, I did. Billy set me up at a table near the stage so he could keep an eye on me. I started out with strawberry daiquiris. The last thing I remember was something called a blue motorcycle."

Sarah grinned. "I bet the next day you were sick as a dog."

"I woke up the next morning in Billy's bed."

Shock filled Sarah's face. "Mom, did he?"

"No," Mary quickly responded, "it was nothing like that. I was still wearing my clothes from the night before. Billy was sitting in a chair watching over me."

Sarah released a sigh of relief. "I thought you were about to tell me that Billy was my father. I bet Dad laughed when you told him this story."

Mary slowly shook her head. "He never knew. I told him that I had driven out to the coast to be alone."

"But why did you lie?"

Mary stared into Sarah's eyes for a while. "You were right." She paused. "I was sick as a dog. I pity the dog that ever felt as bad as I did."

Sarah laughed out loud. "Now I know why you won't drink a drop now."

Mary smiled. "I swore to myself that I would never feel like that again. I was sick the entire next day. Billy stayed by my side the entire time. I saw a side of Billy I never knew."

"That was on Saturday. Didn't Billy have to play that night?"

"He was supposed to. He told his boss that he needed to be off. He told Billy that if he didn't play he wouldn't have a job. Billy chose to stay with me. I felt even worse because he lost his job over me."

"You mean he actually fired Billy."

"Yes. Billy nursed me back to health. It was lunch time on Sunday before I began feeling normal again. Billy treated me like a queen."

"I'm surprised Billy didn't try something."

Mary looked deep into Sarah's eyes. "Billy would never do anything like that. Billy was a perfect gentleman."

"Yes, but Billy's a man. I know how handsy men get when they are drinking."

"He didn't drink a drop."

"Is this the same Billy I know?"

"The same man, just a side you have never met. It was about a year later when Billy began to drink heavily."

"I wonder why." Sarah noticed Mary's hands trembling again. She grabbed hold of them. "Mom, why are you shaking so?"

Mary's eyes began to water, guilt making them overflow. "Sunday afternoon," She paused. "I went to Billy."

Sarah released Mary's hands. Silently she stood up, tears filling her eyes. "No, Mom. No! I don't think I want to hear the rest of this story." She began backing away.

"But, Sarah—"

"No, no!" Sarah shouted as she ran out of the kitchen and up the stairs to her room. She flopped down, face-first into her pillows, crying, because she knew deep down in her heart what the rest of the story was.

7

Sarah hid in her room and cried, trying to escape the truth that was about to spill from her mother's lips, that Billy was her real father and not the man that she had loved her entire life, the only father she had ever known—John. It was hard enough for her to accept that he was really dead; however, to find out that he wasn't her birth father was more than her emotions could withstand. Mary didn't go running after Sarah. She knew that the reality of this news would have to sink in gradually, like soaking a sore wound. Instead, she was going to let Sarah have time to absorb the initial shock before trying to explain any further.

Sarah lay on her bed, trying to cry away her misery. Little did she know, she was not alone. She didn't realize that her buddy was in the room with her. Sarah sobbed face down into her mound of pillows. Her buddy, who was still undetected, could sense Sarah's pain. He decided to make an attempt at cheering up Sarah. He sprang up on the bed, not startling Sarah in the least. By the vibration on the bed she knew exactly who it was—Grayson.

Grayson was a smoky-gray, short-haired cat. He was as plump as a Thanksgiving turkey, about the size of Garfield. The only part of Grayson that wasn't gray was his white chest and four white paws, reminiscent of a cat wearing a gray tuxedo. Grayson began purring as he butted his big head into Sarah's side. He commenced to throwing his body into her as he rubbed against her body. As soon as he made his way up to her shoulder, Sarah snatched him up into her arms, squeezing him as if he was her security blanket. He loved it so much he began purring even louder.

Grayson had somewhat succeeded. Sarah's crying had eased, now that Grayson had made himself the center of her attention. The pain of the truth still weighed heavily on Sarah's mind. She didn't know quite how to deal with this. In many ways Billy was a stranger to her. She wasn't sure how she was supposed to feel, happy that she had a living and breathing father, or angry for no one telling her before now. Questions began to circle within her head, like race cars at the Daytona 500. There was so much she still questioned, like who actually knew of this secret and why was it a secret in the first place. The more she thought about it, the more frustrated she got.

After about an hour, Mary made her way upstairs to check on Sarah. She eased her way down the hall, listening for any signs of life coming from Sarah's room. She stopped at the edge of Sarah's doorway, just out of sight. She could hear Grayson's loud purring, like a motor boat on a serene lake. Mary figured that it may be safe to enter. She stepped into the doorway. Sarah was curled up on her bed with her back facing the door, Grayson securely in her arms.

"Is it safe to come in?"

Sarah hesitated. "Safe for you, but I'm not sure it's safe for me. Do you have any more bomb shells you want to drop on me?"

"No, Darling," Mary answered as she entered and took a seat on the side of the bed. "How do you feel?"

"Confused, angry, you name it. Why, Mom?"

"Why what?"

"Why everything. Why did you do it? Was this your way of getting back at Dad? Why did you wait until now to tell me? That's just a couple questions to start with. How about who? Who knows about this? Who…"

Mary stopped her by placing a hand on Sarah's arm. "Let me tell you the rest of the story. Then maybe that will answer most of your questions."

Sarah rolled onto her back. "Okay, I want to hear all of this."

Mary could see the frustration in Sarah's teary eyes, as well as feel it in her stare. "If you are expecting me to tell you that I'm sorry…It's not going to happen."

"Mom, I can't believe you said that!"

"Just hear me out, Sweetheart. If it hadn't happened the way it did, then you wouldn't be here."

Sarah shook her head. "Don't use that for an excuse. I don't mean sorry for the results. I mean sorry for the act."

Mary gave Sarah a firm look. "I'm not sorry for that either."

Sarah's eyes widened, shock flushing her face. Grayson stepped between them, begging for attention. Mary stroked him gently down his back. "Just let me finish the story." She paused. "This was not an act to pay John back for what he'd done."

"So you were in love with Billy."

Without a word Mary stood and then walked over to the window. Her eyes were drawn out of the glass panes, much like they were in the kitchen earlier. "I'm not sure what to call it." Her thoughts had drifted back in time. "My heart has always belonged to John. But I felt something with Billy that I'd never experienced with John."

Sarah cupped her hands over both ears. "Oh my God…I don't need to be hearing this."

Mary returned to the bed and took a seat. She pulled a hand from one of Sarah's ears. "I'm not going into any details."

"Thank goodness for that."

Mary began rubbing Grayson again. "Then and even today I have deep feelings for Billy."

"Mom!"

"Okay, back to the story. Like I said, this was not a way at getting back at John. It just happened." Her eyes met Sarah's. "And, I made the first move."

Sarah rolled her eyes.

Mary placed her hand on Sarah's forearm. "I had mixed feelings. The passion I felt with Billy didn't outweigh the guilt I was feeling. I knew in my heart that I had to go back home to see if I still had a marriage. I left on Tuesday morning without waking Billy. I left him a note explaining how I felt and what I needed to do." Her eyes fell back on Grayson as she began rubbing him once more. "I went back home to a broken man." She lifted her tear-stained eyes, meeting Sarah's. "John hadn't eaten for over three days. I believe he would have grieved himself to death. He begged me to forgive him." A tear ran down her cheek. "I forgave him. It was easy considering what I had done. And I have never regretted one single day of it. We had a wonderful marriage. You can attest to that."

Sarah wiped tears of her own. "Yes I can. I can only hope to have a marriage as happy as yours."

Mary took Sarah's hand, squeezing it gently. "And together we raised one fine daughter."

Sarah gave Mary a serious look. "He never knew...did he?"

Mary held her stare for a while. "You should've seen John's reaction when he found out I was pregnant. He was ecstatic."

"How did you explain that?"

"Didn't have to. John figured that because of our reunion that an over-excited sperm had made his way through."

Sarah smirked. "And you just left it like that."

"I so wanted to tell him. But after seeing his excitement, I couldn't bear to break his heart."

"And Billy, was he that naïve?"

"No," Mary paused while she thought back. "I think I was about six months pregnant. Billy had started his own band. They had played in Durham over the weekend. He paid me a visit while John was at work. He had done the math. He knew."

"So, that's why you and Billy were arguing the other day. It had nothing to do with a tombstone, did it?"

Mary shook her head. "Back then I had convinced Billy to keep our brief affair a secret. He didn't want to, but I insisted." She smiled. "I really think Billy fell in love with me. Anyway, he went along with it for whatever reason. Probably because he knew that John and I could give you opportunities he couldn't."

"So what were you two arguing about?"

"Billy felt it was time to tell you the truth. John was gone and there was no reason to keep it a secret now. I said no. You are in your third year of law school. I don't want anything interfering with that."

"This is not going to change that. So why have you spilled the beans now?"

"I'm not sure exactly what happened. Your singing this morning flushed out this guilt I've been keeping inside me for years."

Sarah got out of bed and walked to her vanity. Taking a tissue, she wiped her eyes and face. "Now what?"

Mary turned to Sarah. "I guess that's up to you, Darling."

Sarah stared at Mary through her reflection in the mirror. "Me? Why is it suddenly my decision?"

"Well Honey, this is your life. You have to decide where to go from here. And, what role Billy plays in your life."

"What role Billy plays," Sarah repeated as she walked over to Mary and took a seat next to her. "Mom, what am I supposed to feel? What kind of reaction is he expecting?"

Mary patted Sarah on her thigh. "No one is putting pressure on you."

"Maybe not intentionally but I feel like I've been forced into a corner."

"No one is pressuring you. I'm sure Billy isn't expecting an instant daughter that is as close as you and John were." She paused. "When do you plan to tell Billy? He will be coming by in two days. It's almost Christmas you know."

Sarah sprang to her feet. "Mom, I can't face him, not now anyway."

Mary stood facing her daughter. "Tell me what you need to do. I'll help you in any way I can."

Sarah stared into Mary's eyes for a moment. "Would it be okay if I go to the beach house for a few days to sort out my feelings? I'll be back for Christmas."

"Of course, Darling, whatever you need." Mary wrapped her arms around Sarah. "I love you, Sweetheart."

"Love you, too, Mom."

Mary peeled Sarah back, gently, looking deep into her beautiful baby blues and asked, "What do I tell Billy?"

"The truth, Mom…I don't want to be part of any more lies."

8

Sarah packed up and hit the road shortly after lunch. She was headed to Nags Head, North Carolina. They owned a four-bedroom, two-bath cottage located in the family-oriented community of South Nags Head. The cottage sat less than two-hundred yards from the water's edge. Sarah had always loved this area at any time of the year, visiting every chance she got. The atmosphere there was more laid-back than the larger more commercialized beaches. It was even better during the off season. This was the perfect time and place for her to escape. Sarah called Mary the minute she had arrived. There was just enough time left in the day to grocery shop and unpack.

After settling in, Sarah retreated to the back deck with a bottle of wine and a glass. She popped the cork on a bottle of Carolina Muscadine wine. The cottage was built high off the sand, like a house on stilts. Sarah sat and absorbed the cool ocean breeze, perfect sweat suit weather. She sipped on her wine and finally began to unwind. The wine was slowly relaxing her body, but her mind was wandering back home, where she thought she had left her problems behind.

In an attempt to distract her mind, Sarah decided to go inside and curl up with a book that she had purchased to read over the Christmas break. She went inside and secured the doors behind her. She retrieved the book which she had placed on her bed for later. She took it back to the living room, and made herself comfortable on the sofa. Sarah placed her half-empty wine glass on the coffee table and opened the book. She began to read *Safe Haven* by Nicholas Sparks, her favorite author. The combination of the wine and reading pulled at Sarah's eye lids. It wasn't long after she had finished her glass of wine that she retired her weary mind for the evening.

✳✳✳

Sarah woke up early the next morning and attended church. It was the same church she and her parents attended when they spent time here. After church service and a nice lunch, Sarah took her lounge chair, small cooler, and book out to the beach. It was a bright sunny day; however, it was December with a high of fifty-five degrees, perfect weather for Sarah's worn blue jeans and black and gold Wake Forest Demon Deacon sweatshirt. She sat in her lounge chair, soaking up the sun and salty ocean breeze. Normally the soothing ocean breeze, along with the sounds of the waves, had a therapeutic effect on Sarah. Today was much different. Thoughts of Billy being her real father kept sneaking past her defenses. She would pick up her book and begin reading to get her mind off her troubles; nonetheless eventually her thoughts caused her to stare out at the ocean in deep thought.

Sarah's iPhone sprang to life. She was so lost in her thoughts that she completely lost track of time. Glancing at her watch, Sarah knew it was Jessie. She hesitated a moment, because she really wasn't in the mood to talk to anyone. "Hello."

"Hello, Sarah."

"Hello, Jessie."

Jessie could sense distance in her voice. "Did I catch you at a bad time?"

Sarah wanted to say yes; however, she needed a human to talk to. "I'm sorry. I do have a lot on my mind."

"Do you want me to call at another time?"

"No, please don't hang up. I need to hear your voice."

"That's a nice thing to say. I'm glad you wanted to talk. I've been looking forward all week for this time to talk to you."

"Me too, I've had some things to deal with over the weekend."

"I can sense some reluctance in your voice. I know we've known each other for a short period of time, but if you need someone to unload on, please don't hesitate. I'm good at keeping secrets."

Sarah questioned what he meant by keeping secrets. "What secrets?"

"I just mean that whatever you say to me will not go any farther."

"Oh," Sarah said, while wondering if he knew of the secret. "How well do you know Billy?"

"I've known him for six years. Why?"

"Just asking. You seem to be close to him."

"I guess I am. I owe everything to him. He took me in when I didn't have anywhere to go."

Sarah wanted to do a little fishing. "How much do you know about his family?"

"His parents and his only brother have passed. And you are his only niece."

Sarah wasn't satisfied. "Had he ever married or had any children?"

"Where are you going with these questions? It sounds as if you don't even know your own uncle."

Sarah knew that this secret would be out when Billy came to visit. She also knew that Billy would probably tell Jessie if he hadn't already. "You said you can keep a secret."

"That's right. You can tell me anything."

"How do I know you aren't already keeping a secret?"

"You are really confusing me."

"Does Billy have any children?" She blurted out.

The phone went silent for a moment. "You know about Billy's daughter?"

Sarah began to get angry. "I knew Billy must have said something to you. When were you going to tell me?"

"I swore to Billy that I wouldn't tell anyone."

"So you know. How long have you known?"

"Three or four years I guess."

Sarah was boiling mad. "What were you doing, playing me for a fool? Or did you think that just because I'm Billy's daughter that you were going to get in easy with me?"

Sarah cut Jessie off before he could speak, dropping the phone down on top of the cooler. It wasn't but a few seconds before her phone was playing a tune. Sarah stared angrily out at the ocean, all the while ignoring Jessie's call. The phone finally went silent. A minute later Sarah's phone jingled, informing her that a text message had been received. She ignored the jingle. After another minute her phone jingled again, a reminder that the text hadn't been read. It angered Sarah even more. She grabbed the phone to cut it off so she could get some peace. She checked the text first. Shock filled her face as she read his message. *"I didn't know it was you. Billy never said a name."*

Sarah buried her face in her hands, ashamed at the way she had acted. She picked the phone back up and sent Jessie a text. *"I'm sorry."*

It wasn't but a few seconds before Sarah's phone played a tune again. She slowly picked up. "I'm sorry. Please don't hate me."

"Sarah…I could never hate you. I can see how you thought I knew."

"I'm sorry. I think I'm going crazy."

"No need to apologize. Wait a minute. I see now. You just found out yourself."

"Mom dropped the bomb on me yesterday morning."

"Oh my, now I know why you sounded different. Not to mention all those questions."

Sarah took a sip of a diet drink. "My mind is spinning in circles. I'm not sure how I feel or how I'm supposed to feel."

"I'm sure your mother is being very supportive."

"I'm not at home. We have a house at the beach. I came here to sort out my feelings."

"Then I guess your mother is going to tell Billy when he comes for a visit tomorrow."

Sarah sighed. "That's the plan. I told Mom, no more lies. By the way, what and how much do you know? You knew about a daughter?"

"Yes, but never a name. You see, when Billy gets really loaded, he opens up. Years ago he told me about a woman that he was in love with. He never said a name. But she was married and devoted to her husband. He told me that they had a brief affair and that she had his child, a girl. Billy never mentioned any names. I would've never dreamed it was you...except."

"Except what?"

"Billy said that his daughter was very beautiful like her mother. You are very beautiful."

Sarah blushed. "Awww, that's so sweet."

Jessie and Sarah talked for another hour. She released a lot of her emotions. They then talked about Nags Head and the cottage. Along towards the end of their conversation, Jessie sprang a question on Sarah. "Will you go out on a date with me?"

This caught Sarah off guard. "Of course, I'd love to. But when will that ever be? When you are off, I'm at school. When I'm home you are working in a different city every weekend. Are you playing near Raleigh any time soon?"

"We'll be in Greensboro in February. I'll definitely plan something then."

"That sounds great. I can't wait."

"Me either...but just for pretend sake, are you available tonight?"

Sarah laughed. "Okay...as a matter of fact I am. So tell me, how would this first date go?"

"Well…I would show up on your door step at seven with a bouquet of flowers."

"Hmm, nice start, keep going."

"Let me think…I would then take you out to a nice restaurant. You do like seafood, don't you?"

"Love it. Keep going. You're doing great so far."

"Then I will take you for a moonlit stroll along the beach."

"Wait a minute. Where are you going to find a beach in Greensboro?"

Jessie laughed. "Work with me. Remember this is just pretend."

Sarah laughed as well. "Okay, just pretend. So far this is the best date I will never get to go on."

"After we get tired of walking I'll build us a camp fire. We will snuggle up together and count the stars, making a wish before every falling star burns out."

"Make a wish before a falling star burns out. I don't think I've ever heard that one before."

"That's an old, deep southern saying that goes back for generations."

"That's right. We are still pretending."

"Are we?"

They both laughed out loud. Sarah ended the call with a smile on her lips and a piece of her burden off her chest. The rest of the afternoon she couldn't help but wish that February would hurry up and get here, her first date with Jessie.

9

Sarah went out on the deck to enjoy the sunset. The sun was sinking fast behind her, transforming the ocean, in front of her eyes, into an endless sea of red waves. After the sun surrendered to darkness, Sarah spotted lights from a distant ship. She began to reminisce to when she was a child and they came here for vacations. Back then every ship that passed by, in the distance, was a pirate ship destined to some fairytale land faraway, a place she wished she could now escape to, leaving her troubles far behind. Thoughts of her childhood here stirred memories of her parents back then. Sarah recalled all the trips here and how the three ware a happy family. For every good memory she had, there also came a looming question that had never been there before. She tried to picture her life back then with Billy as her father, instead of John.

No matter how much Sarah tried to ignore her thoughts, they kept popping up right in front of her eyes. Thoughts of her mother prompted Sarah to call Mary, another attempt to distract her mind. They talked for an hour about any and every subject not involving Billy. After the call Sarah scratched around the kitchen in search for something to tame her roaring stomach. A knock on the front door caught Sarah by surprise. When she cracked the blind on the window of the front door to see who was at the door, her vision was blocked by a huge arrangement of flowers. Instantly she knew that Jessie must have sent them. She then wondered how he knew the exact address. Sarah settled with the assumption that Mary sent them to cheer her up. When she opened the door Jessie popped his face up over the flowers. Sarah's mouth flew open.

Jessie was grinning from ear to ear. "Surprise!"

"Jessie!"

"We still have a date tonight?"

She stood frozen in disbelief. "Come in. Come in."

"I didn't mean to throw you into shock," said Jessie as he entered.

"You did just that. Where did you come from? I thought you said that you were in Atlanta."

Jessie placed the flowers on the coffee table. "Ahh, I told you that I was from Atlanta. And I also told you that I was visiting my sister, didn't I? I never said where my sister lived. It just so happens that my sister lives near Elizabeth City, a little over an hour's drive from here."

Sarah admired the flowers. "These are beautiful. Thank you." She grinned. "So, you tricked me."

Jessie laughed. "You never asked. So I thought I would surprise you. Don't you love a good surprise?"

Sarah smiled. "I do now."

"Well, are you hungry?"

"Starving."

"Now that's what I wanted to hear. I do believe I mentioned something about seafood."

"You've come to the right place. Give me a minute to change."

Jessie threw her a smile. "You look wonderful like you are."

Sarah looked down at her sweatshirt then rolled his eyes at him. "I don't think so. It won't take me but just a minute."

Sarah changed into a pair of jeans, a white turtle-neck shirt and a baby blue pull-over sweater that matched her eyes perfectly.

"Better?" she asked as she walked into the room.

Jessie thought Sarah was the most beautiful woman on earth. "You clean up nicely."

"Thank you. Now let's hurry before my hunger causes me to turn into an animal."

They both laughed out loud as they exited the cottage. After satisfying Sarah's hunger pains with some shrimp scampi, Jessie brought her back to the cottage. Sarah grabbed an extra wrap and a flashlight. They both headed out to the water's edge. The moon had escaped to the far side of the world, leaving darkness to prevail over the eastern shore. Sarah and Jessie strolled hand-in-hand along the shore using the flashlight to illuminate the path in which they walked.

Sarah was enjoying every minute with Jessie. "Jessie."

"Yes."

"I'll have to admit, this is the nicest first date I've ever been on."

"I was just thinking the same thing. I don't want to spoil the mood but there is something I want to help you with."

Sarah squeezed his hand. "I don't see how you could do anything to spoil this good mood I'm in."

Jessie hesitated. "Maybe another time would be better."

"Come on, Jessie. You definitely have something important on your mind."

"You are the one with something on your mind. And I want to help you."

Sarah stopped. "You mean Billy."

"Yes."

She sighed. "I was trying to avoid this conversation, at least for tonight. I don't see how you can help me with this."

"You had mentioned before how Billy was like a stranger to you."

"He is. I've only seen him about twice a year. All I really know is that he's a singer that drinks a lot." She paused. "That, and the fact that he and my mother had an affair."

Jessie shined the flashlight on a nearby house which appeared that no one was home at the time. He held a constant beam on the house. "Tell me...what do you see?"

Sarah starred at the house for a minute. "Well...the house is grey with a white picket fence around it and a rusted old swing set. No one seems to be at home. The fence needs painting."

Jessie leaned in close to Sarah, his cheek brushing hers. "You are only looking at the outside. Do you know what I see?"

"No, tell me."

"I don't see a house at all. I see a home that a loving couple bought many years ago. They each fixed it up with their own two hands. I can picture the two of them painting that fence when it was new. Later their children brightened their lives and this house as well. That swing set didn't have rust on it then. I see tiny little markings with tiny little names on the door frame to the kitchen. I bet there are tiny hand prints in the cement steps at the back of the house."

Sarah took the light from Jessie's hand and shined it in his face. "Who are you?"

He smiled. "Billy is that house. You only see what's visible on the outside. I see Billy for who he is on the inside, a part you have never seen."

She glanced back at the house. "I can't help what I see."

"I understand. I can tell that this is hard for you. I am not going to pry or try to force you to open up. I just want you to know that I'm here for you. If you want to talk about Billy or ask questions about who he really is...then who better to talk or ask than someone who knows Billy from the inside?"

Sarah wrapped her arms around Jessie. "Thank you. That is so sweet."

He kissed her on her forehead. "Let's head back now. I need to start that campfire I promised."

They turned back, strolling hand-in-hand along the shore, retracing their footprints. Thoughts of what Jessie had just said stirred in Sarah's thoughts. "How did you meet Billy?"

Jessie thought for a moment. "I was eighteen. I had just left home and was headed to Nashville to be a star. I had a hundred and twenty dollars to my name. I was at a truck stop to hitch a ride to Nashville."

"That was a crazy idea."

"Maybe…but I was desperate and that was the only way I could afford to get there. Billy was there eating with some men. I didn't know at the time that it was his band. He must have noticed my guitar case and struck up a conversation with me. I told him where I was headed. I thought he might have been a truck driver. He wanted to hear me play. I told him that I couldn't play in the truck stop in front of these people. That's when he asked me, how was I going to play in Nashville if I couldn't play here in front of these strangers? Billy told me that if I would play for him, then he would take me to Nashville. I still thought he was a truck driver."

"I take it you played."

"Played my little heart out."

"You must have impressed him."

"Looking back on it now…I was pretty bad. I'm still not sure what he saw in me or why he asked me to join his band. But I'm sure glad he did."

"Billy didn't get you to Nashville."

"Maybe not, but I wouldn't have made it there anyway. Billy took me under his wing. He taught me how to play and sing better."

The darkness didn't reveal Jessie's misty eyes. "Billy has been like a father to me. He is more of a father to me than my real father ever was."

They continued along the beach, conversing in small talk as they strolled along. Sarah didn't bring up the subject of Billy anymore.

She wasn't ready to completely open up to Jessie quite yet. Once back at the cottage Jessie began working on the campfire while Sarah went inside to get a blanket for them both to sit on. Sarah returned with a blanket, a bottle of wine, and two red Solo cups. After the campfire was able to burn on its own, Sarah and Jessie snuggled up on the blanket near the fire. The night sky was clear, with millions of bright stars shimmering brilliantly. Every once in a while when Jessie stirred the fire, fiery red embers would rise into the sky, as if mingling with the stars above. Sarah and Jessie sat dangerously close to one another, a warm red glow from the fire reflecting off their faces.

"I brought us some wine," said Sarah as she took out two cups.

"No need to pour me any. I don't drink."

Sarah wore a surprised expression. "You really don't drink?"

"Nope...I have seen what alcohol can do to you."

Sarah tucked the cups away. "Oh, I'm sure you have."

"I know what you're thinking...but it's not Billy I'm referring to. Alcohol mellows out Billy. It has the opposite effect on my father. It brings out the evil in him. And I was usually there in his way when it did. If there is the slightest chance that alcohol may have the same effect on me, then I don't care to partake in it. I've been through enough hell growing up. But go ahead and have some. Don't let me stop you."

"That's okay. I'm not a big drinker anyway."

They both looked up at the stars. Sarah nestled up even closer to Jessie. "Are all you band members like sailors, a different girl at every port?"

Jessie laughed. "Is that what everyone thinks? That may be true for some, especially the ones who make it big. But I'm too busy. I'm Billy's agent as well."

"You're kidding."

"Nope. Not long after I was in the band, I could see how Billy's agent was ripping him, and us, off. So I deliberately got in close with the agent and learned the business very quickly. It wasn't hard. I became friends with all the owners. Then I approached Billy with the idea of me becoming a working agent. I showed Billy how he was being cheated out of a lot of money. He fired the agent and ever since then I have been too busy to think about girls." He paused. "That is until the day I met you."

Sarah smiled. "You are full of surprises."

Jessie leaned in close, whispering into Sarah's ear. "I feel the need to give you fair warning."

"Fair warning?"

"Yes…I should warn you that I will easily fall in love with you."

"What makes you so sure?"

He leaned closer, his lips brushing her ear. "Because I fell in love with you many times before."

Sarah cocked her head, her eyes meeting his. "What?"

"Yes, it's true. Over the years when Billy had too much to drink, he would pour out his heart. He told me everything about you except for your name. The first time he mentioned you…the way he described you. I'm not talking about your outer beauty. It was the way he described your inner beauty that made me fall in love with you the first time."

Sarah stared deep into his eyes, both sparkling like the stars above. Like magnets, their lips met. After a sweet seductive kiss she positioned herself even closer to him than she was before.

"I have a confession to make."

Sarah looked up into his eyes and smiled. He returned her smile. "I've had plenty of opportunities in the past where I could've stopped Billy from drinking past his limit."

"So why didn't you?"

"Because I knew that each time Billy got loaded, he would talk about you. Then I could fall in love with you all over again."

Sarah felt an irresistible attraction while staring deep into his eyes. "If you don't stop," she sighed, "you won't be the only one falling."

Their lips met again.

10

Billy arrived at Mary's house an hour past lunch. Mary had been expecting him. She met Billy at the door. As always, Billy came bearing gifts. He wasn't aware that his greatest gift was waiting for him this Christmas, the news that Sarah had finally been told the truth, that he was her real father.

Mary opened the front door. "Merry Christmas, Billy."

"Merry Christmas, Sugar."

Mary greeted Billy with a kiss on his cheek. To her surprise Billy didn't show any signs of drinking, not even on his breath. She led him into the living room where neatly wrapped gifts were waiting.

Billy's eyes wandered about the house. "Where's the little princess? I didn't see her car outside."

Mary ignored the direct question for now. "Have a seat, Billy. May I get you something?"

Billy laid his gifts on the coffee table. "I thought I detected fresh-brewed coffee. A cup would be nice."

"Coming right up," said Mary as she exited for the kitchen.

The house was quiet, with the exception of Mary stirring about in the kitchen. Billy leaned back on the rustic-brown sofa, his eyes drawn to the mantle filled with pictures in gold frames. He stared at John's portrait for a minute. It was as if John was staring back at Billy. Feeling a bit uneasy, Billy's eyes drifted down the mantle, landing on Sarah's. It was a graduation portrait of Sarah dressed in blue and wearing a big wide smile.

Billy was so drawn by Sarah's smiling face that he rose and walked over to the mantle. He lifted the picture from the mantle, gazing into Sarah's beautiful face, as thoughts ran uncontrollably through his mind.

Mary entered with two cups of coffee, noticing his stare. "That has to be one of Sarah's best photos. Her expression really reflects her true personality. Don't you agree?"

"Some people can never take a bad picture," said Billy as he eased the picture back into its proper place.

Mary stepped closer, handing him a cup. She quickly turned, avoiding eye contact.

Billy noticed her strange behavior. "You never did say where Sarah was at."

Mary walked to the other side of the room. She stood gazing out the window. "I usually sleep late on Saturday mornings. For some odd reason I couldn't last Saturday. So I came down the stairs. Sarah was in the kitchen doing the dishes." She took a sip from her cup, her eyes fixed through the window. "She had the radio turned up. Carrie Underwood was singing Jesus Take the Wheel." She turned to Billy, her eyes filling with tears. "Sarah was singing right along with Carrie note for note. I couldn't tell the difference. Billy...that girl inherited her talent from you."

Billy sat down quickly on the sofa. He deliberately sat with his back to Mary so she couldn't see his teary eyes. Mary walked over and took a seat close to Billy.

Billy turned his tear-stained eyes to hers. "Mary, please—"

Mary stopped him by placing her hand tenderly over his lips. "There's no need in asking me to tell Sarah the truth. I was so moved by her singing...that I just had to tell her everything that happened."

Billy broke down on Mary's shoulder. She shed tears and held him tight while he released years of bottled up emotions. After a couple of minutes, Billy pulled away, wiping his tears with a hand. "I'm sorry."

"Sorry...sorry for what?"

Billy couldn't make eye contact with Mary. "A grown man is not supposed to cry like a baby."

"Don't be silly. I know this has been hard on you for years."

He finished wiping his face dry with his hands. "You have no idea how much I've longed for this day to come."

She took him by the hand. "I know. That's my fault. I had always believed that it was best for Sarah if John and I raised her. But when I heard her singing, it made me wonder if I did the right thing after all." She could feel Billy's hand trembling. Her eyes fell on his hand. "Are you all right?"

Billy stood quickly. "I need a cigarette to calm my nerves. I'll be back in a minute."

Once Billy had escaped through the front door, Mary moved back near the window. She watched Billy from a distance. He had a cigarette lit before stepping off the front stoop. Even from this distance Mary could see that his nerves were on edge. He paced back and forth while inhaling the cigarette in hardly a minute. Before his lungs could get free from smoke, Billy lit another. He then made his way to his vehicle. Billy opened the passenger side door and went straight for the glove compartment. Mary watched as Billy turned up a bottle that was still within a brown paper bag. When Billy finished his second cigarette, Mary went to the sofa and took a seat.

Billy came back in and took a seat by her. "Okay, Sugar... please tell me how you told her and what her first reaction was."

Mary looked into his eyes. "You had something to drink, didn't you?"

"Just a little. Just enough to calm my nerves."

"I can remember a day when you didn't drink so much."

"Mary…not now."

"When did you let the alcohol take control of you?"

"You really can't remember?"

"No, should I?"

"Do you remember the first time I visited after Sarah was born?"

"Vaguely…I remember you came while John was at work."

"You never liked it when I did."

Mary didn't answer. She just stared into his eyes, which was an answer enough for him.

Tears began filling his eyes. "When you laid that precious little girl in my arms…I can't explain it, but it touched my heart deep down. I would have changed my life completely, just to be a part of hers. Just knowing that I would never be a part of her life was more than I could bear. That's when I turned to alcohol to deaden the pain."

"Billy."

"Please, change the subject. Tell me how you told her and how she reacted."

"I heard her singing. As I listened to her, I just felt guilty for keeping it a secret all these years. When she noticed me, I was standing in the doorway crying. She thought the song was bringing back memories of John."

"If John was still here we wouldn't be having this talk right now."

Guilt pulled her eyes away. "Probably not…I don't know." She looked back into his eyes. "That's when I told her the whole story."

"Even John's affair?"

"Yes, I didn't leave anything out."

"I know that must have hurt the both of you."

"It was the hardest thing I've ever had to do." She paused. "With the exception of burying John."

"And Sarah?"

"She ran to her room crying."

Billy slowly rose to his feet. He eased over to the mantle, staring at Sarah's smiling face within a frame. "So that's why she's not here. She hates me now."

Mary went to him. "Billy...she doesn't hate you. She is confused. You have to understand what she's going through. Just three months ago she lost the most important man in her life, John. Now, to find out that he wasn't her real father after all, truly put her into shock!"

Billy turned to Mary. "I'm not trying to replace her memories of John."

"I know."

"I am thankful of how you and John raised her."

"I know that."

"He will always be in her heart. I'm fine with that." He paused, tears returning to his eyes. "I just want Sarah to find a little place in her heart for me."

Mary hugged him. "She will, Billy. It will just take some time."

11

Meanwhile in Nags Head, the morning began with a late breakfast on Sarah's patio, overlooking the ocean as the morning sun was slowly rising. Jessie had spent the night in the guest bedroom. The beach campfire lasted to the wee hours of morn. Later in the middle of the afternoon, Jessie and Sarah were once again walking the beach, hand-in-hand, as they did the night before. The cool ocean breeze nipped at their cheeks. Never the less the two endured the punishment, both equally loving the beach at any time of the year.

Jessie would stop every once in a while, taking Sarah's hands within his cupped hands. He would blow his warm breath on her hands to keep them from going numb.

"So how did your sister end up in Elizabeth City?"

Jessie gently blew his warm breath on Sarah's frigid fingers. "I have an aunt and uncle that live in that area. They were never able to have children. So every summer my sister, Sally, and I would spend the whole month of July with them. They own a cottage up at Kill Devil Hills. Sally, who is a year older than me, met someone here when she was a senior in high school. After college, they married and settled down near Elizabeth City."

"So that's how you found me so easily."

"I know every inch of this beach, from here to Kill Devil Hills. It was my summer escape."

They began walking again. "Escape? You sound as if you were in prison."

"More like a prisoner of war camp."

Sarah looked up at Jessie. His serious eyes were cast out over the ocean. "That bad?"

Jessie stopped. He turned to Sarah, a look of pain in his eyes. "Do you remember me telling you how alcohol brought out the evil in my father?"

"Yes."

"It was every night. He was a cop…still is I guess."

"You mean you don't know?"

"No. My sister and I never speak of him. He is dead in my eyes."

"Jessie, you don't mean that!"

Jessie took her hands, warming them with his breath once again. "Run your hands under my sweatshirt. Feel my back."

Sarah slowly ran her hands under his sweatshirt. The warmth of his back felt like a heating pad on her cold hands. As she ran her hands up his bare back, she felt rough places. "What is this?"

"He beat me with a belt…the buckle end of it."

Sarah quickly spun him around, lifting his sweatshirt from the back. Jessie's back was filled with scars. Her eyes began filling with tears. "Oh, Jessie…what kind of monster could do this?"

"A drunken cop who brought his work home with him every night."

Sarah's eyes overflowed with tears. She began gently kissing his scars. Jessie could feel her warm tears running down his back. He slowly turned to her. He took his hands and wiped her tears away.

Sarah looked up into his caring eyes. "What about your sister?"

"He never touched her. I made sure of that."

Jessie kissed Sarah on her lips. They held each other for a while. They began walking again, their arms around each other's waist.

"How old were you when it started?"

"Fourteen...about six months after Mom died from breast cancer."

"I'm sorry you had such a rough childhood. Didn't your aunt or uncle see the scars and ask questions?"

"Not at first. I wore a shirt as much as possible to hide my scars. When they finally noticed, I lied. I told them the scars were from a dirt bike accident." He paused. "You are the only one I've told the truth to."

"Your sister knows the truth."

"Yes, it's our little secret. At the time we were too afraid of what he was really capable of, especially being a cop. Now, it doesn't matter. He is out of both of our lives now. We asked our aunt and uncle not to tell him of our whereabouts. They were very suspicious of why, but promised anyway. They know he has a mean streak."

They strolled along the beach, and then took a well-beaten path back to Sarah's cottage. They went to a local restaurant for dinner, where they enjoyed succulent crab legs. Their table had a large window that gave them a picturesque view of the ocean at sunset. After dinner they retreated to Sarah's cottage.

"Would you like another campfire beneath the stars?" asked Jessie as he held the front door for her to enter.

"Let's stay in tonight. It's a bit colder than it was last night. We can cuddle up and watch a movie."

"That sounds like a winner to me." Jessie noticed a half-empty bottle of wine on the counter. "And just because I don't drink doesn't mean you can't."

"I know...I just don't want any. I don't drink to get high. I like the taste of some drinks."

"What do you like the best?"

"Well, my favorite is a strawberry daiquiri. But I also like sweet wine and apple martinis. As a matter of fact I do make a great strawberry daiquiri. I picked up the stuff to make daiquiris."

"That sounds good. I'll have a strawberry daiquiri."

Sarah wore a confused expression. "I'm not going to give you a mixed drink. I remember what you said."

Jessie raised a finger. "No, I want a virgin daiquiri."

She smiled. "That I can do. How about you cut up the strawberries."

He returned her smile. "I think I can handle that."

Sarah opened the refrigerator and brought out a plastic container filled to the brim with red juicy strawberries. She handed him a small thin knife and a cutting board. Jessie began capping and slicing the strawberries, while Sarah pulled out the blender and the other ingredients.

"Tell me…what is it like at Wake Forest?"

She smiled. "It's amazing. The atmosphere is like no other place. I'm sure everyone thinks the same way at their school, but the students and faculty at Wake Forest are great."

"Isn't it a party school?"

"Not really. I mean they all are to a certain degree. It depends on who you hang out with, and how serious you are about an education." She paused. "Myself, I plan on graduating at the top of my class."

"I bet you will."

"So far I'm in the running. It has taken a lot of hours studying, not partying." She stopped and smiled. "I do close the books one night a week. That's on Friday nights. A group of my friends and I go down to a local bar and grill. Friday night is karaoke night."

Jessie stopped cutting and looked at her. "Karaoke?"

"Yes, we all have a ball. But that is the only night I give my brain a rest."

He began cutting strawberries once again. "So…do you get up on stage?"

"Sure I do. Most all of us do." She began laughing. "Some of them are clowns. We all laugh our heads off. It's a great time. I really miss it."

"What about you?"

"What do you mean?"

"Do you clown around…or are you good?"

Sarah wouldn't make eye contact. "I try my best. It's all for fun."

His interest had peaked. "What do you sing?"

"Various songs…country music, of course."

"Which is your favorite?"

"There are many. But there is one that I would have to sing every Friday night. Everyone looked forward to it."

"What was that?"

"Strawberry Wine."

"Deana Carter."

Sarah smiled. "That's right. The crowd loved it."

"Sing it for me."

She blushed. "You don't want to hear me sing. Anyway, I don't have the music."

"Oh, come on…please. You don't need the music. Sing acapella."

She shook her head. "I don't know if I can. I might scare you away."

"That's impossible. Pretty please. I told you a secret that I haven't told anyone else…not even Billy. So the least you can do is sing for me."

Sarah looked into his eyes. She could see that he was serious. A smile crept across her face while a mischievous look filled her eyes. She picked up a dish towel from the counter top and placed it around her neck like a shawl. She began moving toward him as she began singing the chorus. She stepped close to his side and dragged the dish towel across the back of his shoulders while singing the next line. She leaned into him, looking up into his eyes, flirting as she sang on. She threw her arms around him, coming face-to-face while finishing the chorus. She kissed him and began laughing out loud.

Jessie smiled. "That was good."

"The kiss?"

"No silly." He shook his head. "Yes the kiss was good. I was talking about the singing."

"It's all for fun. Nothing serious."

"I want more."

She smiled at him. "More kisses?"

He smiled back. "That too, but I'm talking about the singing."

"That's all I got. Anyway, I'm too busy making us drinks."

Jessie returned to his task of cutting strawberries. "Who is your favorite singer?"

"There are so many I like. But if I had to pick one…it would be Carrie Underwood."

"Do you sing any of her songs?"

"Of course. As a matter of fact I was singing one when Mom walked in on me and dropped the bomb."

Jessie noticed her expression change when she said, bomb. He knew it was the news about Billy, a subject he wanted to avoid. "What was the song?"

"Jesus Take the Wheel."

"Wow, that's a great one."

Sarah looked at his bowl of chopped strawberries. "I am ready for those berries. What's taking you so long?"

He smiled while he went back to work. "I'm almost done. You don't rush perfection."

She planted her hands on her hips. "I don't need perfection. I'm going to obliterate them anyway."

"You make it sound so horrible."

She laughed. "You are silly. Just hand them over."

Sarah dumped the strawberries into the blender with her mixture. Jessie watched her as she blended the drink. "Do you have the CD?"

"What CD?"

"Carrie Underwood's CD with "Jesus Take the Wheel" on it."

"Yes…why?"

"I want to hear you sing that song."

She began pouring the virgin daiquiri into two tall glasses. "I've already sang you a song. I thought we were going to watch a movie."

"You only teased me with a chorus. And that was acapella. I want to hear you really sing. Then we can watch a movie...I promise."

She shook her head. "I can see that I'm not going to get any peace until I sing for you."

"Like you said, it's just for fun, nothing serious."

"I don't know if I can sing in front of you without laughing."

"I tell you what. I will stay in here. You go into the living room out of my sight and sing your little heart away. Pretend I'm not even here."

"Okay, I'll try."

Jessie took a seat in the kitchen while Sarah went into the living room just out of his sight. He could hear her searching through CDs. Then he heard her turn on the CD player. All was quiet for a long moment. Then the music began. When Sarah began to sing, Jessie was caught by surprise. She was singing note for note with Carrie. Sarah nailed the high notes in the chorus as well. Jessie was overcome by her performance. As the music was ending, Jessie entered the living room wearing a smile.

Sarah smiled. "I see you're still here."

"Sarah, that was awesome. You have some real talent there."

"You sound like my mother."

"I'm serious. You should sing with the band."

Her eyes narrowed. "I'm sure Billy would love that. No thank you. I am going to be a lawyer. I have a job waiting for me when I graduate."

Jessie could see the seriousness in her eyes. He also knew that Billy was a sore subject at this time. He walked up close to Sarah. "Well, Baby, you can sing to me anytime you want."

His sweet gesture softened her mood. Their eyes locked and they melted into a kiss.

12

The next day was Christmas Eve. That morning Sarah headed home while Jessie returned to his sister's home. When Sarah arrived the house was empty. According to an earlier phone conversation, she knew that Mary had gone to the grocery store for a few last minute items before the doors closed for Christmas. Sarah entered the living room where to her surprise the family Christmas tree was standing and decorated. She wondered how her mother could have figured out how to put it together. It had always been a task for John, one he enjoyed every year. The tree was an artificial Balsam Spruce pine, standing eight feet tall that looked very real. Mary had decorated it the way Sarah had always remembered it.

Sarah stood staring at the tree as memories flooded her mind. She envisioned John putting the tree together piece by piece, all the while humming to Christmas carols on the CD he had playing. She pictured the three of them decorating the tree. The tree was filled from top to bottom with bright and shiny ornaments. Every year they would go out and buy a new ornament for the tree, sometimes signifying an event that had happened that year, such as Sarah's high school graduation. It hadn't dawned on her, until this moment, that she and her mother hadn't bought an ornament for this year. She questioned if this would be the end of this particular family tradition, since John was no longer present and the fact that it was getting too late to go out and purchase one. The thought of this tradition ending saddened her. Sarah's life had changed so much in the last several months.

Sarah's sad thoughts were broken by the sound of someone pulling into the driveway. She pulled back the curtain, seeing that Mary had arrived. When Sarah turned back, her eyes fell upon a certain gift under the tree that shouldn't have been there. She approached the tree and picked up the package. Just as she suspected, it was the gift that Mary had wrapped for Billy from Sarah. Sarah wondered if Billy had come by and why Mary had failed to mention it.

Mary came through the door with bags in hand. "Hello, Darling, I sure have missed you." She took notice of Sarah's puzzled face. "What's wrong?"

Sarah raised the present. "You didn't tell me Billy never came."

"That's because he did come," Mary responded, then hurried to the kitchen.

Sarah placed the gift back under the tree, then tracked Mary to the kitchen. "Why didn't he open his gifts?"

Mary began putting away the groceries, intentionally ignoring Sarah.

"Mom," Sarah stretched out the word, "don't tell me Billy is going to be here tomorrow."

Mary finally made eye contact. "Of course not, Darling. He knows this is our first Christmas without John. He doesn't want his presence to interfere with our thoughts and memories of John." She paused a long moment while looking deep into Sarah's eyes. "He did ask if he could come by the day after Christmas."

Sarah rolled her eyes, planting a hand on her forehead. "Oh, Mom, I bet you said yes."

"What could I say?"

"You could have said that now is not a good time. That's one good answer. I can think of a few more."

"You can't hide from Billy forever."

Sarah flopped down in a chair at the kitchen table, her eyes staring across the room in thought. "I know."

"You know that you will be seeing much more of Billy now than in the past."

Sarah sat in thought. "I know...especially now."

Mary noticed Sarah's distant stare. "What do you mean by that?"

Sarah turned her stare toward her mother. "I think I'm falling in love."

Mary's eyes flew open. She hurried to the table and took a seat close to Sarah. "How did we get off track from talking about Billy to you falling in love?"

Sarah smiled. "It's not that far off track. I think I'm falling in love with Jessie."

"I only met him once, but he seemed like a nice young man. But how do you fall in love just by talking on the phone? That is what dating is for."

"We've been on a couple of dates already."

A confused expression popped up on Mary's face. "Where was I when this happened?"

"Right here. He surprised me at the cottage."

"At the cottage?"

"He is spending Christmas with his sister who lives in Elizabeth City. When we were talking on the phone I told him where I was and why. We talked about having our first date. He even described what it was going to be like. I thought we were pretending. He's from Atlanta and that is where I thought he was. Instead he surprised me by showing up on my front door step."

"You had two dates?"

"Yes...yesterday and the day before. We ate some great seafood. We spent a lot of time talking while walking the beach. We even had a campfire beneath the stars."

"That sounds romantic." Mary began rubbing her chin in thought. "So let me get this straight. You and Jessie were alone at the cottage for two days."

"Mom, he spent the night in the guest room."

"Oh, well that is good," Mary said, a bit relieved.

"The first night."

Mary's hands shot over her ears. "Oh my! I didn't need to know that."

Sarah laughed as she pulled Mary's hands from her ears. "Isn't that what you were driving at?"

"Yes, I guess. You are twenty-one. That makes you an adult. John and I raised you properly. I have all the confidence in the world that you will make good decisions—"

"Mom!" Sarah said, interrupting her. "Don't get all bent out of shape. Everything is fine. Yes I was raised properly. I take this very seriously."

Mary took Sarah's hand. "I know you do, Dear. This is just new to me. You have always kept your mind on your studies... not boys."

"That's right. And that will not change. I won't be able to see him very often. So that works out well with my studies."

"Now I know what you were talking about. The more you see Jessie, the more you will be spending time with Billy as well."

"Yes, exactly! Mom, I still don't know what I am supposed to feel about Billy. Yes, he's my real father, but he's still a stranger. I had a real father all my life, until now. I can't just switch my feelings like that."

"I know, Honey. I understand completely."

"But, does Billy understand that?"

Mary smiled. "Billy is a very understanding and caring man. You just haven't seen that side of him. He understands what you are going through better than you think."

"So, the two of you talked about me, huh?"

Mary squeezed Sarah's hand. "We talked about a lot of things, including you. He's not expecting you to suddenly treat him like a long lost father. All he wants is to be a part of your life... Whatever part you can spare. With his schedule and yours, it can't be much time. Just take it one day at a time. That's all he's doing. And that's all he can hope for."

"Okay, one day at a time. So, he's going to be here day after tomorrow, right?"

"Yes, you and I will have Christmas Day alone, together."

Sarah remembered about the ornament. "Mom, I hope we can continue with some of our family traditions, even though Dad is not with us."

"I wouldn't have it any other way. And, I'm sure John would want us to."

Sadness filled Sarah's face. "I wish we could have gotten a Christmas ornament this year. That was something I always looked forward to."

Mary smiled as she patted Sarah on her hand. "I have something to show you."

Sarah watched as Mary went hurriedly into the living room. When she came back, she was carrying a small plastic bag and handed it to Sarah. "I picked this up yesterday afternoon." She paused, giving Sarah a warm smile. "I hope you approve."

Sarah slowly opened the bag. She reached in, pulling out a square golden box. She lifted the lid. Inside, resting on a bed of cotton was an ornament in the shape of two hands cupped. Cupped hands represent Father God's hands, openness to receive the love of God.

Mary placed a tender hand on Sarah's shoulder. "I thought that this would be fitting...since John is in God's hands now."

Sarah's eyes watered, a single tear broke free and was streaming down her cheek. "I love it, Mom. It's perfect."

13

Christmas Day was very quiet and private for Sarah and Mary, fitting since it had only been three months ago they were burying John. They spent part of the day at John's grave, a new family tradition in the making. With no close relatives living, the only other contacts Mary had were a few of her church friends. Sarah had a quick call from Danielle, and an extensive one with Jessie. Sarah told Jessie about Billy's visit and the plans for a Christmas feast on the day after Christmas. That was when she decided to ask Jessie to come too. It was her attempt at breaking the uneasy feelings she had of meeting Billy face-to-face for the first time as father and daughter.

The next day began bright and early with Sarah and Mary in the kitchen. A Christmas feast was another family tradition they both thought had been laid to rest with John. Preparing for this meal rekindled a piece of the Christmas spirit that had been lost. Sarah was busy helping Mary, but her mind was on the awkward encounter she had to face when Billy arrives. She smiled at the thought of Jessie arriving at the same time as Billy, her plan of escape from the uncomfortable meeting with her new father.

Mary took notice of Sarah's smile. "It's good to see you smiling…penny for your thoughts."

"I can't wait to see Jessie, that's all."

Mary smiled as she continued with her work. She already knew of Sarah's little plan, and why she was doing it. Mary, being a devoted mother, knew what was best for her daughter. Being a woman experienced in life, she had her ways of making things happen for the best, without her daughter realizing what was happening. Just as the meal was coming all together, the sounds of gravel popping beneath tires broke Sarah's concentration. Mary pretended she didn't hear a thing. Sarah glanced up at the clock as she thought to herself. *"It's only a few minutes after twelve. Who can that be?"*

Mary smiled to herself as she noticed Sarah rushing toward the front door. Sarah returned as quickly as she left, her face flushed in shock. "It's Billy. He's early."

Mary didn't raise an eye. "No…he's right on time."

Sarah began to panic. "But I told Jessie to be here at one."

Mary's eyes rose, meeting Sarah's. "I know. That's why I told Billy to come earlier."

Sarah's eyes flew open. "Mom—"

Mary cut her off. "Sarah, you need a few minutes alone with Billy before Jessie steals your attention."

"But Mom—"

"I know," said Mary, cutting her short once again. "I messed up your little plan." A warm smile grew on her face. "Now why don't you go greet Billy? I can finish up in here."

Sarah watched Mary turn toward the oven, checking the rolls. "I never knew you could be so sneaky."

Mary peeked in the oven, her eyes only on the rolls. "I love you, Sarah."

Sarah sighed as she turned away. Mary cut an eye her way, then smiled as she watched Sarah head toward the front door to greet Billy. Sarah reluctantly walked to the front door, her anxiety growing from within with every step. She stopped at the front door and took a peek through the glass pane. Billy was just making his way onto the front sidewalk, outfitted in blue jeans and jacket to match. Beneath his jacket was a red shirt. His black cowboy boots matched the cowboy hat on his head.

Sarah finally got up the nerve to open the front door and step out onto the front porch just as Billy was topping the steps. "Hello, Billy, Merry Christmas."

"Hello, Sugar, and a Merry Christmas to you."

They stood face-to-face for a moment, as if both were waiting for the other to speak. Sarah was not aware that Billy was just as nervous as she. He didn't show it because the whiskey he had earlier was keeping his nerves calm.

Billy finally opened his arms. "Do I still get a Christmas hug?"

Breaking the ice, Sarah smiled as she surrendered into his arms for a hug. She had always greeted him with a hug in the past, but this time felt strange to her, a feeling she couldn't explain.

"Where is Mary?"

Sarah released her hug. "She's hiding…I mean she's busy in the kitchen."

Billy grinned, knowing well what she meant. "So, your mother threw you out to the wolves or wolf should I say."

Sarah grinned. "Something like that." She pointed to the outdoor furniture on the porch. "You want to sit for a while?"

"Okay, Sugar," Billy replied as he took a seat.

Sarah took a seat. She began fidgeting, obviously uneasy. Billy couldn't help but notice her nervous behavior. "Sarah—"

"Billy," said Sarah before Billy could say another word. "Can I say something first?"

"Why sure, Sugar."

Sarah got up from her chair and eased to the railing. After a moment of gathering her thoughts, she turned to him. "Billy, I don't know…I mean I'm not sure." Her words became tangled. Frustrated, she quickly turned back around.

"Sarah, I know this is hard on you. It would be a lie if I said I know how you feel. Because I don't, not exactly. I know how I feel, and what I've felt the last twenty-one years. So why don't we do this. You tell me what you are feeling and I'll tell how I have felt over the years."

Sarah slowly turned around, her eyes watering. "That's just the problem. I have mixed emotions about the whole thing."

"That's understandable, Sugar. We have something in common. So let's start here. Would one of those emotions be anger?"

"Yes," Sarah blurted out. "That was my first reaction. I was mad at you and Mom for keeping this secret from me all my life."

"I've been mad at Mary about it for twenty-one years."

Sarah wiped her eyes. "But you went along with it."

"I didn't want to." He paused. "But your mother can be very persuasive. And if I didn't go along with it then, I would risk losing you both."

"She says it was for the best."

"And, she's probably right. You've turned out to be a fine young woman. I have Mary to thank for that...and of course John."

Sarah's eyes watered once more. "That's where I'm having more mixed emotions. He was the only father I've ever known. I can't change the way I'll always feel for him."

"I know that, Sugar, and I don't want you to, even if you could. I'm eternally grateful to John for the way he loved you and raised you. But...since we are exposing feelings, I'll have to admit that I've been very envious of John for years."

"But you still kept quiet. Why?"

Billy slowly rose and stepped to the railing by Sarah. "Look around. What do you see?"

Sarah looked around then gave him a confused stare. "I don't know what you want me to see."

"I want you to see the same thing I do. It is exactly how Mary pictured it when you were born. I couldn't see it then, but I do now."

"See what?"

"I see a lifestyle I could have never provided for you and Mary. This nice home and another at Nags Head to start with. Then making enough money so Mary could quit her nursing job and stay home. And then sending you to college. I couldn't have given you all this, even if I had taken a stable job instead of singing in clubs."

"So, Mom was right all along."

"Please don't tell her I said so. She's probably listening in on us anyway."

Sarah smiled. "It wouldn't surprise me a bit."

Billy turned to Sarah, his eyes filling with tears. "Sugar, I have something I want to say now. I have loved you with all my heart from the first day I cradled you in my arms."

Sarah quickly turned away. "Billy."

"I had to tell you how I've felt all these years."

She turned to Billy, her eyes overflowing with tears. "That's the problem. I don't know how I'm supposed to feel or what you expect me to feel. That is what's driving me crazy."

Billy placed a comforting hand on her shoulder. "Sugar, I'm not expecting you to feel a certain way. I know that you are not going to instantly accept me as your father. That I hope will come in time, probably a long time if ever. We will take it one day at a time. All I want, all I'm hoping for, is a little place in your life. Your life is not going to change. You are going to be a great lawyer someday. I just want you to be happy."

Sarah hugged Billy. "Thank you."

Jessie was coming into the driveway. Sarah quickly peeled herself off Billy, leaving him standing alone trying to figure out what had just happened. Sarah ran down the sidewalk to meet Jessie. Mary came through the front door, timing it perfectly.

Billy smiled at Mary. "I guess you heard all of that."

Mary returned his smile. "I heard enough. You did good, Billy...real good."

Billy turned his stare toward the driveway, spotting Jessie's car. "Didn't know Jessie was coming. Who invited him?"

"I'll give you one guess."

Billy raised a brow at the sight of Sarah and Jessie locked in a kiss. "What is this? Have I missed something?"

"Evidently…they've been talking regularly for several weeks now."

Billy kept staring. "That's a little more than talking as I remember it."

Jessie and Sarah made their way up onto the porch, their bodies glued together. Jessie locked eyes with Billy. "Hey, Pop."

Billy grinned. "I sure hope you've been using good manners when around a lady."

Jessie smiled. "Just the way you taught me, Dad." He turned his stare toward Mary. "It's nice to see you again, Mrs. McCray." He kissed her on the back of her hand.

"Oh my," said Mary with eyes wide open.

Billy smiled wide. "That's my boy."

They all laughed out loud.

Sarah's anxiety suddenly dissipated the moment Jessie arrived. The talk she and Billy had before Jessie arrived greatly helped her uneasiness. The four sat down to a delectable meal.

"So, how was your stay at Nags Head?" Billy asked while his eyes were on a slice of turkey he was cutting.

"Wonderful," Jessie spit out without thinking.

Billy cut his eyes toward Jessie. Jessie, realizing what he had just done, dropped his eyes to his plate.

Sarah choked on her food while giving Mary a wild look. "Mom!"

Mary sniggled. "I haven't breathed a word."

Jessie looked at Sarah. "Oops."

Sarah and Jessie chuckled, with Mary quickly following suit.

Billy eased his forkful of turkey back down to his plate. "I must have missed something else."

"Well, Billy," Mary said after a swallow of water, "while you and I were having our Christmas get together the other day, it seems that Sarah and Jessie were getting better acquainted at Nags Head."

"It was all my idea," said Jessie while smiling at Sarah.

"Is that so?"

Jessie cleared his throat. "Yes it was. After Sarah had agreed to our first date, I surprised her at the beach. She had no idea I was anywhere near Nags Head. She thought I was calling from Atlanta."

"So that explains the show you two put on."

Sarah's mouth flew open. "What show?"

"The two of you lip locked in the parking lot. I thought I was going to have to hose the two of you down."

Sarah blushed. "Oh, Billy."

Billy laughed. "I'm just messing with you, Sugar." He turned his stare to Jessie. "So the two of you had your first date?"

Jessie smiled. "Actually our first and second date." He turned his eyes to Sarah. "And now I'm hoping she will accept my offer for our third date."

Sarah sighed. "When will that be, next Christmas?"

"How about Valentine's Day?"

Sarah's face lit up. "Valentine's Day?"

Jessie took her hand. "The band is playing in Greensboro that weekend. I want you to be there. Then we can spend all day Sunday together."

Sarah squeezed his hand. "I would love that."

Jessie turned to Mary. "Better yet, why don't you come along too, Mrs. McCray?"

"Oh…I don't know."

"Come on, Mom," Sarah said excitedly. "You need to get out the house for a while."

Billy looked over at Mary. "I would love for you to come. You have never heard my band."

Mary locked eyes with Billy for a moment. "I'll think about it…I promise."

14

Christmas passed, and so came the birth of a brand new year. Sarah returned to school where she buried herself in her studies. Even with her busy schedule, she made time to talk to her mother every day. The two had always been close, their bond strengthening with John's passing. Sarah continued to come home every weekend. Jessie called Sarah several times a week, a love gradually blossoming like a flower in spring. Thoughts of Billy crept into Sarah's mind on a regular basis. She was still unsure of what type of relationship she would have with him, if any with her new father she didn't really know that well. She couldn't see past his drinking problem.

Remnants from the storm that took John's life were beginning to surface. Gradually, Sarah's life was changing, like the leaves in fall. These subtle changes were slowly steering Sarah into her own fate's path.

***

Valentine's weekend had finally arrived, none too soon for Sarah. She had finally convinced Mary to get away for the weekend. They drove separately to Greensboro, because Sarah was to return to school, after her date with Jessie on Sunday. Sarah and Mary planned to spend Saturday shopping, and then watch Jessie and

Billy perform that night. Sarah booked a room for her and Mary on Saturday night, after the show. The plan was for Mary to drive back alone on Sunday because Sarah and Jessie were going to spend the day together, their third date.

Saturday evening, after a nice afternoon of shopping and dinner, Sarah and Mary headed out to Black Jack's where the Billy the Kid Band was playing, the very same place Mary stumbled into twenty-two years before, while escaping John's little affair. Billy had a table nearest the stage reserved for them both. When Sarah and Mary entered, it was already packed. The waitresses all were wearing pirate attire, and the house special drinks were rum, of many assorted mixtures. With only twenty minutes until show time, Mary and Sarah got two virgin daiquiris and headed to their table.

A few minutes later Billy made his way to their table to greet them, his face filled with a wide smile, as his eyes landed on them both. "How are my two favorite girls doing tonight?"

Mary returned his smile. "We are doing great."

Sarah's eyes were bouncing around the room. "Where's Jessie?"

"He's back stage preparing for the show, Sugar. He takes his work very seriously. Me? I say let's just play." Billy's eyes fell on Mary's drink. "Mary, what are you drinking?"

Mary picked up the glass and took a sip through the straw. "A strawberry daiquiri."

Billy's eyes widened with surprise.

Mary began laughing. "A virgin daiquiri."

Billy released a sigh of relief. "I thought if that was the real thing, I was going to call 911 in advance."

They both laughed out loud. Billy glanced at his watch. "If I don't get back there now Jessie's going to have my hide. I sure am glad the two of you are here. We have a great show in store for you two."

Billy disappeared backstage. A few minutes later a tall thin man made his way to center stage while Billy's band took their places behind him in the shadows.

The tall thin man took a microphone in hand. "Welcome everyone to Black Jack's, Happy Valentine's Day. It's my pleasure to introduce you to The Billy the Kid Band. I suggest you get a dancing partner fast because you're in for a treat tonight. Great country music love songs is the theme for tonight."

The lights remained dim on the band while a lone spot light shown down from the ceiling on Billy. He was sitting on a stool with an old guitar in hand. His head was tilted down, his cowboy hat shadowing his face. Billy slowly raised his head as he began singing George Jones' all-time great "He Stopped Loving Her Today." The dance floor quickly filled while Billy sang perfectly in a voice as smooth as silk.

Sarah was surprised, drawn by his pleasing voice. "Mom, he sounds great."

"He's gotten better with age. Now you see where your talent came from."

"Mom," Sarah said, about to scold Mary for that remark. As she stared at her mother, Billy's suave voice captivated Sarah, to where she couldn't help but think about the reality of Mary's statement.

"I have a cassette somewhere that he recorded years ago," Mary continued. "I think it wasn't long after he formed his own band. I don't remember him sounding this good."

Sarah's eyes turned back to Billy, looking past the alcohol for the first time, breaking down a portion of the protective barrier she had formed. "He's good. I'm very impressed."

The crowd erupted in cheers as Billy finished the song. The spotlight then moved off Billy and onto Jessie. Sarah's face lit up the same moment Jessie's did. They made eye contact and shared a smile.

Jessie positioned himself in front the microphone, an electric guitar in hand. "There is a special someone in the audience tonight I wish to sing this song to."

Everyone knew who he was speaking of just by just following his eyes. Jessie began to sing another all-time great from another legend named George "I Cross My Heart" by George Strait. The lyrics spilling from Jessie's lips melted Sarah's heart. Jessie could tell by Sarah's glassy eyes that he had moved her. What he didn't realize was that Sarah had just fallen madly in love with him at this very moment. Mary spotted the glow on her daughter's face right away. She smiled, watching Sarah absorb his words.

Billy and Jessie took turns singing classic country hits, some older and some most recent. Nearing the end of their first set, Billy made eye contact with Jessie and smiled. He then turned to the drummer and nodded his head. The band began playing a familiar and very popular tune.

Billy stood middle stage, staring out at the crowd. "I have one more song I want to play before we go to break. It's only fitting that since we are doing classic love songs that we play this one. Does anyone recognize this tune?"

"Strawberry Wine," came from the crowd.

Billy pointed a finger from where the answer came. "That is correct. But we have a problem. Though I know the song by heart, I don't think it would sound right with my voice." He turned to Jessie. "Do you think you can do it, Jessie?"

Jessie shook his head while playing the tune over and over. "I don't think so, Billy. What are we going to do? We can't stop the song now."

"You're right, Jessie." Billy turned back to the audience. "This is when I wish we had a female vocalist."

Sarah turned to Mary. "Mom, what's going on?"

Mary patted Sarah's arm which lay on the table. "I have no idea. Why are you asking me?"

Sarah raised a brow. "Because, I know you."

Billy stood with a puzzled look on his face. "If only we had a volunteer."

Mary grabbed Sarah around her wrist and shot her arm up in the air. Billy spotted it right away. "There we go, Jessie, a volunteer."

Sarah jerked her arm down, stabbing Mary with a pair if surprised eyes. "Mom! Why did you do that?"

Billy smiled. "Go get her, Jessie."

Jessie made his way to Sarah's table, her eyes still locked on her mother. "Come on, Sarah."

Sarah wanted to say no, but all eyes were on her. "What are you doing?"

Jessie took her by the hand as she rose to her feet. "Nothing serious, just some fun."

"I don't know if I can do this," Sarah said as they stepped up on stage.

Jessie sat a microphone in front of Sarah in center stage. "Sure you can. You've been doing this at that karaoke bar."

"That was in front of my friends."

Jessie looked into Sarah's eyes. "They are all your friends here. If I didn't think you could do this, I wouldn't have put you up here."

"So this was your idea."

He kissed her on her cheek. "Yes. We will begin when I get into place."

Jessie quickly returned to his spot and nodded to Billy. The band began playing the song from the beginning. Sarah stood frozen, looking out over a room filled with strangers. No one at this point was paying her any attention. They were all back at their tables drinking and laughing with each other. Anxiety began taking over Sarah, as she stared out at the unconcerned crowd. The point for her to begin had passed her twice. Billy locked eyes with Jessie and tilted his head in Sarah's direction. Jessie went to Sarah's rescue.

Seeing the fear in her eyes, Jessie stepped between her and the audience. "What's wrong, Sweetheart?"

"I can't do this. Look around. They aren't even acknowledging that I am up here."

Jessie placed a tender hand on her chin, pulling her eyes to his. "It is always like this, no matter who is on stage. Trust me. They will acknowledge you once you begin to sing."

"But they are all strangers. I've only sang in front of my friends."

"Let's try this. Look around through the crowd until you see someone that reminds you of a friend back at school. Focus on that person and your mother. It will work."

Jessie gave her a reassuring kiss then returned to his spot. Sarah began canvassing the crowd. She spotted a young woman nearby with red streaks in her hair. Thoughts of her best friend, Danielle, popped into her mind, easing her tension a bit. Then a mountain of a man rose out of his seat a few tables back. His bald head reminded Sarah of Rock, the owner of the karaoke bar where she sang. Sarah felt her anxiety lifting as she looked into Mary's smiling face.

Sarah turned to Jessie and smiled. He motioned to the band to start at the top. Sarah fell in on cue. As soon as Sarah began to sing, one by one the audience turned their attention to the angel on stage. Two by two they filtered onto the dance floor as Sarah sang the first chorus. Jessie looked over at Billy, whose teary eyes were glued on his daughter, a sight he had never dreamed he would ever witness. Billy could feel Jessie's stare. He turned and gave him a quick smile. The audience exploded in applause as Sarah finished the song. Jessie ran up and gave her a hug.

Billy was drying his eyes. "We are going to take a break now."

Jessie helped Sarah back to her table where Mary sat in tears of joy. It wasn't long before Billy came to the table with the tall man that made the introduction on stage at the beginning of the show. "Sugar, there is someone who wants to meet you. This is Jack Holloway, the owner." He turned to Mr. Holloway. "This little lady is Sarah McCray."

Mr. Holloway took Sarah's hand. "It is a pleasure to meet you. That was some performance. What relation are you to Billy?"

The question stunned Sarah. It was the first time she had been asked publicly where she had to think about it. "Daughter, I'm his daughter," she said, tripping over her words.

"Where have you had training?"

"My only training has been at a karaoke bar."

Mr. Holloway had a surprised expression on his face. "Then you must have natural talent. Thursday night is karaoke night. I would love to hear you sing here."

"I'm afraid that's not possible. I'm a student at Wake Forest."

"My loss. How about a few more songs tonight?"

Sarah shook her head. "Thanks, but I don't think I can. The band is not familiar with the songs I know."

"That's not a problem. Like I said, we do karaoke. I can set you up during a band break."

"Are you serious?"

Mr. Holloway took out his wallet and pulled out three crisp one-hundred dollar bills. "Very serious…"Strawberry Wine" was one of my wife's favorite songs. I lost her to cancer a year ago. I haven't heard anyone sing that song the way you just did. How about three songs during the next band break? That's all I'm asking."

The story of his wife touched Sarah's heart. She pushed his money back. "Did your wife have another favorite?"

Tears filled his eyes. "Jesus Take the Wheel."

Sarah smiled. "That's one of my favorites, too. You got a pen and paper?"

He handed her a pen and paper and she scribbled something down. "Give this to your DJ…in that order. I'll do it on the next break."

"Thank you," Mr. Holloway said as he glanced at the list. "Oh my God!" He raised his eyes to meet hers. "Thank you again. Food and drinks, whatever you want is on the house."

Jessie watched Mr. Holloway leave a happy man. He turned to Sarah. "What did you put on that list?"

She smiled at him. "Maybe I'll sing you a song. Do you know his wife's name?"

"Angela...she was a real nice lady."

Billy, Jessie and the band went back to work. They performed more great love songs from yesteryear and today. When it came time for a break, Billy and Jessie traded places with Sarah.

Mr. Holloway stepped up to the microphone on stage. "Okay folks, while the band is taking a break I have a treat for you. You already know her face and that great voice from earlier. I take pleasure in introducing Sarah McCray, Billy the Kid's daughter."

The crowd clapped as Sarah stepped up to the microphone. "This first song I would like to sing in memory of Angela Holloway."

Sarah nodded to the DJ. The music began and Sarah sang "Jesus Take the Wheel." She removed the microphone and walked about the edge of the stage, singing out to the audience like she did on karaoke night at Rock's. All of her anxiety from before had vanished, like a thief in the night. Sarah was in her zone, hitting every note perfectly. Billy watched his daughter perform on stage, tears filling his eyes. Mary noticed his glassy eyes. She placed a comforting hand on his forearm which was resting on the table. Billy turned his eyes to hers, giving her a smile. He placed his other hand on top of hers as he turned his attention back to Sarah. The audience clapped and whistled at the end of her performance.

"Thank you," Sarah said to the crowd while motioning to the DJ to hold up. "This next song has always been a favorite of mine. I would like to dedicate this one to the late great Whitney Houston."

Sarah began to sing a great Dolly Parton hit that Whitney Houston made immortal "I Will Always Love You." She had the crowd mesmerized at her raw talent. The dance floor was filled with lovers. At the end of the song, the crowd roared once again with applause.

"Thank you so much," Sarah said with a smile as she held up a finger to the DJ. "This last one I'm about to do is for someone special here tonight."

As soon as the music began, the crowd exploded in cheers. Sarah smiled wide at the audience, and then began singing "How Do I Live (Without You)," an unforgettable hit by LeAnn Rimes. Sarah removed the microphone from the stand, singing out to the audience as if they were all close friends. About half way through the song Sarah locked her sights on Jessie, and slowly drifted his way. Jessie met her stare, soaking up her words as if she had written the song for him alone. His love for Sarah had been slowly flourishing over the past couple of months. Sarah singing directly to him drove his heart over the edge, falling madly head over heels in love with her at this moment. By the end of the song she was standing at the edge of the stage near him. She reached out for him as she sang the last lines. Jessie stood and took her free hand.

Sarah smiled into Jessie's eyes after the final lyric. "I love you, Jessie Beckman."

Jessie leaped up on stage and into Sarah's arms. "I love you too, Sarah McCray."

They sealed their love with a kiss.

15

The following morning, Sarah and Mary had a nice breakfast together before Sarah was off with Jessie on their all day date. Mary checked out of the motel on her own just before 11 a.m.. Once she got into her car to head home to Raleigh, she decided to call Billy to thank him for a wonderful show last night. She had told him once after the show, but Billy was pretty well intoxicated and she didn't know if he remembered it or not.

Billy picked up on the third ring. "Hello."

"Billy, how are you feeling this morning?"

"Just fine now, Sugar. Are you on your way home?"

"Just about to leave. I just wanted to thank you for last night. I really enjoyed the show, and I know Sarah did too."

"Sugar, I should be the one thanking you. It meant the world to me having you and Sarah at the show."

Mary recalled the look in Billy's eyes when he watched Sarah sing. "I know. I could see it in your eyes."

"Yes," Billy said, then paused. "I want to talk to you about something."

"Okay."

"If you're not in a hurry, can we meet for lunch?"

Mary thought for a moment. "I guess we can. All I have is an empty house to go home to."

"Do you know where the mall is?"

"Billy," Mary said, stretching out his name. "I'm a woman. Of course I know where the mall is."

Billy laughed. "How about meeting me at the main entrance in about forty-five minutes?"

"Sounds good."

Billy picked up Mary and took her to a nearby restaurant. Once they ordered and got comfortable, Mary gave Billy a serious eye. "You wanted to talk about something?"

"Yes, it's about what Jessie is going to ask Sarah today."

Mary's eyes popped open. "Question?"

"No, not that question. But they are in love. I guess you could see that last night."

Mary smiled. "Yes, and I couldn't be happier. They make a nice couple."

"I think so too. The problem is they don't get much time to spend together."

"That's true, but what can they do?"

"Jessie came up with an idea. I'm all for it, but I'm not sure if Sarah will or how you would feel about it."

Mary looked puzzled. "About what?"

"Jessie wants Sarah to join the band."

Mary shook her head. "No, Billy. Her education is more important, and I'm sure Sarah feels the same way."

"So do I. I agree one hundred percent. Jessie is on board with us."

Mary's confused stare returned. "So why is he asking?"

"Only during the summer. Jessie is going to ask her to sing with us during her summer break."

Mary leaned back in her seat. "Oh, that's different."

"This way the two love birds can spend more time together." Billy smiled. "And she can get to know me better."

Mary matched his smile. "That would make you happy, wouldn't it?"

"It would be a dream come true. How do you feel about it?"

"I think it would be great. Especially after seeing her perform last night. But it's not my decision. Sarah is a grown woman now. She will have to follow her heart."

"What about you? How about you come along too? Just for the summer. Did you have a good time last night?"

"Yes."

Billy's face lit up. "So you will come this summer?"

Mary shook her head. "Yes, I had a good time last night. No, I'm too old to go traipsing around the country."

"Mary, you are not old."

"I'm no spring chicken either. Anyway, Sarah might say no."

"And if she says yes?"

Mary thought about it for a long minute. Billy kept a constant stare on her, hoping she would say yes. Mary finally met his stare. "I'm willing to go to some, like I did this weekend. Not halfway across the country either. I would definitely consider the east coast, no farther than Atlanta."

Billy smiled wide. "That would be great. This is going to be one great summer."

Mary raised a finger. "You don't know what Sarah's going to say. She might be turning Jessie down as we speak."

✳✳✳

Meanwhile, Sarah and Jessie were walking hand-in-hand in the Carolina SciQuarium at the Greensboro Science Center. This was the first time there for either of them. Sarah and Jessie marveled at the schools of fish swimming right up next to the glass, as if they were tame.

Sarah pulled Jessie close. "How is it that you come up with the best dates?"

Jessie smiled. "So far it's been luck."

"How can it be luck?"

"I hope this doesn't sound selfish, but I have been doing things I wanted to do. I have wanted to come here for a long time."

"Me too."

"Walking the beach, that's one of my favorite things to do, whether its day or night, hot or cold."

"Mine too. I could live on the beach."

Jessie began shaking his head. "Oh no! We have a big problem."

"What problem?" she asked, taking him seriously.

Jessie looked deep into her eyes with a serious stare. "We are not supposed to like the same things." His eyes widened. "That means we might be compatible."

She punched his arm. "You silly, I thought you were being serious."

Jessie laughed out loud. "I am being serious. What happened to opposites attract?"

"That's just an old saying. Yes, opposites can attract, but the couples that have a lot in common have the more meaningful and lasting relationships."

Jessie cut her an eye. "And you are an expert in this field?"

Sarah stared off into the blue water. "I think I am." She paused. "I saw it every day in my parent's relationship." Sarah grabbed her head with both hands. "That is, John and Mary."

Seeing her frustration, Jessie wrapped her up in a hug. "John and Mary are your parents. John was your father in every sense of the word."

Sarah buried her face in his chest. "I know. I just don't know how to react sometimes. I have a father who is dead and gone, and another that is still a stranger to me."

"I'm sorry you're going through all of this."

Sarah looked up at him through teary eyes. "It's not getting any better. If anything, it all just got worse."

His eyes narrowed. "How is that?"

"I have fallen in love with a man who will also be a stranger in my life."

He pulled her tight. "What if I told you I could fix that?"

Sarah pulled back, looking up into his eyes. "How can you fix that?"

He smiled. "We were good last night, but you were the star of the show."

She pulled back farther, shaking her head. "There is no way I'm quitting school to…"

Jessie placed a finger tenderly on her lips. "You are not quitting school. I am a firm believer in getting an education. My life is not glamorous, even though I love what I do. There have been many times I wished I had toughed it out with Dad and gone to college."

"Then what are you trying to say?"

He took her by the hand. "I want us to be together over your summer break. This would not interfere with your school. You already see how we do it now. Billy sings a song, and then I sing a song."

"It really sounded good last night, especially the opener Billy sang."

"You're right. The crowd went crazy over that song. But like I said before, you were the star of the show. You brought down the house when you performed your three songs."

Sarah smiled, recollecting the moment.

Jessie pointed at Sarah. "You can't tell me that it didn't make you feel good."

"No, I can't. It felt really good. And it was fun, that's all."

Jessie held his hands out. "That's right, and that's all it will be this summer, just fun. What do you say?"

"I imagine Billy is all for this."

"I wish you could have seen the look on his face."

Sarah thought back. "When?"

"The first song you sang, Strawberry Wine." Jessie's eyes swelled. "That was the first time I have ever seen Billy cry."

Not sharing his feelings, Sarah took him by the hand, trying to redirect his thoughts. "This would be just for fun, that's all, right?"

"Of course not," He quickly responded. "I'm serious about this. Sarah, I love you, and want to spend as much time as possible with you."

Sarah smiled as she fell into his arms. "I love you too, Jessie. I want to be with you as much as I can. It does sound like a lot of fun, too."

Jessie pulled her back, a hand on each of her shoulders, excitement in his eyes. "You know what I would really like?"

"No, what?"

"I would love to do some duets with you."

Her face brightened. "Duets?"

"Yes, like the one with Jason Aldean and Kelly Clarkson "Don't You Wanna Stay.""

"I love that one."

"How about Clint Black and Lisa Hartman "When I Said I Do." Or Brad Paisley and Carrie Underwood "Remind Me.""

"Jessie…you don't play fair."

Jessie smiled. "I got it. My all-time favorite, Tim McGraw and Faith Hill "Let's Make Love.""

"That does it. How can I say no now? But don't forget the number one by Kenny Rodgers and Dolly Parton "Islands in the Stream.""

Jessie wrapped both arms around Sarah, spinning around in a circle, thrilled. "Yes, that one too. We are going to have the best summer ever."

16

The next three months rolled right on by, wrapping up another long year of school for Sarah. Jessie made time in his busy schedule to get Sarah moved back home. They spent the following two days with Mary, then off to Baton Rouge, Louisiana for Sarah's first performance with the band. Weeks before, Sarah had given Jessie a list of songs she knew by heart, all she had performed on a regular basis, when she used to go with her friends to Rock's on karaoke night. While Sarah had been finishing up her last weeks of school for the year, Jessie had been working with the band to incorporate the list of songs that Sarah had given him.

Sarah and Jessie arrived early at the club, The Cajun Queen, a combined restaurant and night club, owned by an old friend of Billy's, Mr. Schumacher. When they entered, Billy and Mr. Schumacher were at a table enjoying mixed drinks.

Mr. Schumacher stood to greet them. He was a tall, broad-shouldered man with coal-black hair, apparently dyed by the touch of silver trying to escape along his hairlines.

He greeted Jessie with a wide smile and a firm handshake. "Jessie…it's good to see you." His eyes fell upon Sarah. "And this must be Sarah."

Jessie turned to Sarah. "Sarah, this is Mr. Benjamin Schumacher, the owner."

"It's nice to meet you," Sarah said as she gave him her hand.

Mr. Schumacher took her hand gently, as if handling a delicate flower. "It's my pleasure. Please, call me Ben."

"Big Ben," Billy remarked.

Mr. Schumacher cut Billy an eye and grinned. "That's Big Ben for you, old man," He turned to Sarah. "But your beautiful daughter can call me, Ben."

Sarah was having a hard time getting used to being referred to as Billy's daughter. She wondered what Billy had told him, since they were apparently good friends. She masked her uncomfortable feelings with a smile. "Don't worry, Ben. I don't pay him any mind."

Ben let out a big laugh. "I like you already. Please, order anything you wish. Dinner is on me."

"Does that go for the old man, too?" Billy asked, humorously.

Ben looked in Sarah's eyes. "Do you think I should let him eat for free?"

Sarah grinned, playing right along. "I'd make him wash some dishes."

Ben leaned in closer. "I might just do that."

They all laughed out loud.

Come show time, Ben stepped up on stage and introduced the band. He also announced the new addition, Billy's daughter, Sarah McCray. Jessie looked over at Sarah and smiled an attempt to ease her anguish from the introduction. She returned his smile but Jessie could see the uneasiness in her eyes. He was in tune with Sarah's feelings, an advantage of being in love with her. Just knowing that Jessie was by her side helped Sarah cope with the tension she felt inside.

Billy kicked off the show by singing an old Willie Nelson song, "Blue Eyes Crying in the Rain." This was an oldie but a goody, which pleased the crowd according to the applause received. Sarah was up next. She could feel the stares from the crowd weighing down on her. She knew that the first performance was like a first impression, and had to be perfect. Sarah started off strong by singing a popular Shania Twain song "Whose Bed Have Your Boots Been Under." The crowd took to Sarah instantly, and she to the crowd. She felt comfortable on stage, like she had when singing karaoke. Billy watched proudly as his grown-up daughter pranced across the stage, singing confidently to her captivated audience.

Jessie had organized the show where Sarah would sing two songs in each of the four scheduled sets. Sarah was on her way to stealing the show when she sang her second song of the night. She chose a song from a singer who shares her same singing style. The audience was moved when Sarah sang a heartbreaking Martina McBride song "Concrete Angel." Sarah knew she had moved the audience by the many who were wiping tears from their eyes as they listened to the words, probably visualizing in their minds the music video and the meaning of the song. Sarah finished the song and received a roaring ovation. The next song was supposed to be Jessie's, but the crowd cried for more from Sarah.

Jessie motioned for the band to hold up as he approached Sarah. "Let's give them what they want. Which song do you want to sing next?"

Sarah could feel the emotion in the audience. She decided to give them another moving song. She whispered her choice in Jessie's ear.

He smiled. "Great choice." He then went over to Billy and then to the band to inform them of Sarah's song choice.

Sarah tilted her head forward, closing her eyes as she stood center stage, ready to perform this next song in a way that would catch Jessie off guard. Sarah's choice was "I Will Always Love You," performed Whitney Houston style. Sarah remained poised until the crowd quieted down. Sarah gradually opened her eyes as she slowly raised her head. Just like Whitney, Sarah began the song without music, her voice crystal clear and vibrant, much like

Whitney's. The dance floor was full, but most was motionless; all eyes were drawn to Sarah's performance on stage.

When the band came in for the chorus, the audience roared. Sarah slowly walked along the edge of the stage while singing out to her new fans. When the song came to its last chorus, Sarah turned, locking her eyes with Jessie's. She sang directly to Jessie, as she walked toward him. The audience began to react to her move, whistling and applauding as she closed in on him. Jessie, following his heart, met her center stage. They stood face-to-face, staring into each other's eyes as she finished the song, topping it off with a tender kiss.

Seeing the reaction from the audience, Jessie had an idea of his own. It was his turn to sing, giving Sarah a much needed break. He rushed over to the band and to Billy, letting them know of his song change. Sarah was unaware of his thoughts or the song change. Sarah slipped behind the band to take a sip of water from a bottle. The band began to play. It wasn't the song Jessie was supposed to sing. She lowered the bottle and turned an eye toward Jessie. He was smiling at her while motioning with his finger for her to come.

Sarah couldn't quite remember the tune, though the music sounded very familiar. She smiled as she approached Jessie. He held out his right hand while smiling back at her, his eyes sparkling in the lights. Just as their hands connected, Jessie began to sing "I Swear" by John Michael Montgomery. His act caught Sarah by surprise, just as she did him with her song. The audience didn't know that it wasn't a planned part of the show. The women squealed when Jessie began singing to Sarah. Inside, Sarah wanted to squeal herself, but kept her composure for the show.

Jessie stared right into Sarah's eyes as he sang. After a few verses, Sarah was moved by the way he sang to her, as if he had written the song for her. At first she thought it might be just for the show. As Jessie was getting into the second chorus, Sarah noticed his eyes getting misty, letting her know that he was really singing from his heart. Sarah's love for Jessie was growing with every word, and too was his love for her. Jessie ended the song with a seductive kiss, driving the audience wild. Seeing that the two love birds were caught up with each other, Billy made the announcement that the band was taking a break.

During the rest of the show, Jessie and Sarah sang to each other when it suited the song, pleasing the crowd. By the end of the show Billy was really soaking up the booze. At the end of the last set, Billy could barely walk. Sarah watched as Jessie helped Billy backstage. It was apparent to Sarah that this was probably a regular occurrence. Billy's drunkenness didn't alarm Jessie or the other band members. Jessie tended to Billy as if it was part of his job. Sarah followed them backstage where Jessie placed Billy on a sofa.

Sarah approached Jessie. "Is he always like this?"

Jessie peered over at Billy, who had flopped over on the sofa. "Some days it isn't this bad."

"Some days!" Sarah remarked as she stared at Billy. The sight of him in this state sickened her. "Why do you do it?"

Jessie sensed her anger. "If it were John, wouldn't you help him?"

"That's not fair. John was the only father I've ever known."

Jessie pointed at Billy. "And he has been like a father to me. So I am going to help him any way I can."

Sarah was getting angrier the more she looked at Billy. "I didn't sign up for this. He may be blood, but not a father to me." She began shaking her head. "I don't think I can do this. Maybe I should pack up and go home."

Jessie stepped closer, blocking her view of Billy. "You can't keep running."

She looked up at him, anger filling her eyes. "Running...what do you mean running?"

"Billy is your father. When are you going to accept that?"

She pointed toward the sofa. "I don't have to accept that, now do I?"

"So you just want to run away."

"That's what you call it. It's more like getting away from him to me."

Jessie's eyes turned sad. "So…you want to get away from me?"

"No, Jessie."

"That's what it sounds like to me. What about the show we just put on?" Jessie's eyes began to water. "For your information, I meant every word in that song I sang to you."

Sarah recalled his misty eyes when he sang to her. "I know. I felt it. I meant the words I sang to you." She fell into his arms. "I love you, Jessie. Me leaving is not going to change that."

"So you are going to leave."

Tears began running down her cheeks. "I don't think I can be around him. I'm sorry."

A silent moment passed.

"I envy you," Jessie said, breaking the silence.

Sarah pulled back and looked up into his eyes. "What do you mean you envy me?"

Jessie stared at her with serious eyes. "Billy is your father by blood. I only wish he was my blood father. You don't realize how great a man he really is."

Sarah rolled her eyes. "Now you sound like Mom. She has told me that there is a side of Billy I haven't seen."

"She's right."

Her eyes narrowed. "C'mon now. Billy seems like a nice person when he's sober. But all I can see is a drunk lying on a sofa."

"That's because you are looking with your eyes only. You have to open your eyes and heart as well. Then you will see the great man your father is."

Sarah looked around Jessie at Billy out on the sofa. "I can't see what you and Mom see. I can't be around him."

"Twenty-four hours."

Sarah turned her stare back to Jessie. "Twenty-four hours?"

"That's right. You've only been here one day. Give Billy one more day."

"I can't see how one more day is going to change anything."

"You said you loved me."

Her eyes softened. "Of course I do, but my love for you is not going to change the way I see Billy."

"If you love me…then promise me on your love that you will not leave tonight."

"Jessie."

"I'm serious. Promise me."

"Tomorrow is Sunday. Don't we have a date?"

Jessie hesitated. "Yes."

"You said that like you weren't sure."

"Yes, I'm sure. I just thought of something."

Sarah smiled. "What are you up to?"

"Is that a promise or not?"

"Yes, Jessie Beckman. I promise on our love that I will stay one more day."

17

On Sunday, Jessie took Sarah out for lunch. They were both enjoying a salad when Sarah looked up at Jessie. "I missed you last night."

He smiled. "I missed you, too. I'm sorry."

Sarah was still bothered about Billy's drunkenness. "It's okay. You're not to blame. By the way…how is Billy this morning?"

Jessie wiped his mouth then looked into her eyes. "He's fine. I know you are still upset about last night."

Sarah dropped her eyes into her salad bowl. "I'm not upset with you. I thought about it. And I remember what you told me about your real father. I can see how you might look up to Billy. He did help you out when you needed it."

Jessie smiled while shaking his head. Without a response, he returned to eating his salad.

Sarah caught the expression on his face. "What kind of look is that?"

Jessie checked his watch for the third time in the last ten minutes. "You say you understand. But you really don't." He smiled. "You will. You'll see."

She watched him chew his food for a minute. "I didn't want to start this day with a heated discussion about Billy."

His eyes quickly rose. "Then don't." He held his stare for a moment then smiled softly. "Just enjoy this time we have together. Everything will work itself out."

Sarah's eyes narrowed. "Jessie Beckman...you're up to something."

He painted on a fake, shocked expression on his face. "Who, me?"

"Don't you give me that innocent look. I know you are up to something. Why do you keep checking the time? Is it because you are running out of time? Your twenty-four hours is rolling right on by."

He chuckled. "Trust me, my love. I am not worried about the time. When I get through with you today, you won't remember anything about last night."

After lunch, Jessie drove Sarah through the city. She didn't question him on where they were headed. Instead she enjoyed the sights along the route through Baton Rouge. He turned into the entrance to the hospital.

Sarah turned to Jessie. "You said Billy was fine, didn't you?"

"Yes...Billy is fine."

Sarah watched as Jessie turned into the parking lot for the children's wing. "Children's hospital? Do you have a child you haven't told me about?"

Jessie laughed out loud. "No, Sarah. If you must know, a friend of mine has a granddaughter here. She has cancer. I would like to stop in and see her."

"That's so sweet."

"We don't have to stay but a minute...unless you decide you want to stay longer."

They walked into the hospital hand-in-hand. As they walked through the halls, Sarah couldn't help but glance into the rooms as they passed. Children of all ages and races occupied the rooms, lying in beds, some at death's door. Sarah was filled with compassion for the children, asking the same question we all ask

God in our thoughts, *'Why the children?'* Jessie sensed Sarah's distress by the troubled look on her face. He didn't say a word, but only smiled.

Jessie suddenly stopped. He turned to Sarah, taking both of her hands in his. They were standing in front of double doors leading into the auditorium.

Sarah looked around, confused. "Why are we stopping here?"

Jessie smiled wide. "I want you to see what I see on a daily basis."

He began walking backwards toward the doors, pulling her along with him. Sarah was still confused. Jessie pulled Sarah up to the double doors. He cracked one side open, letting Sarah take a look inside, undetected. A small stage was on the far end of the room. On that stage, sitting in a chair, was Billy with an old guitar. He was surrounded by children while he sang "Puff the Magic Dragon" to them. There were family members, doctors, and nurses sitting around listening as well. There were children of all sizes and colors sitting around Billy. All their eyes and ears were glued to Billy as he sang tenderly to them all.

Sarah looked upon Billy in a different light. No longer did she see the drunken man passed out on the sofa the night before. Instead, she saw a loving and caring man who thought more of others than himself, reminiscent of the man she used to call dad—John. Sarah was overcome with emotion. She stepped back out of the doorway, leaning back against the wall. She shut her eyes, squeezing out tears.

Jessie wrapped his arms around her. "Are you okay?"

"I can't believe my eyes. That is the sweetest thing I've ever seen."

"Yes it is. It takes a special kind of man to do that." He paused. "Wait a minute. Was that Billy on stage?"

She punched his arm. "You set me up. Why didn't you tell me?"

Jessie gently lifted her chin to where their eyes met. "You wouldn't have had the same reaction if I had just told you about it. This is the Billy McCray your mother and I have been telling you about, a caring and compassionate man. This is the man I would proudly call my father."

"But you lied to me."

"I'm not a liar."

"You said that a friend of yours has a granddaughter here."

He took her hand. "That's the truth. And you know who it is. C'mon."

Jessie led Sarah through the double doors. Ben Schumacher greeted Sarah with a hug. "Sarah, I'm glad you could come." He turned and pointed toward Billy. "Do you see that little angel in pink by Billy? That's my granddaughter."

Sarah looked at the little girl in pink, about six years old she guessed. Her head was as slick as a peeled onion, an apparent side effect from chemo treatments. She had a baby doll clutched tightly in her arms. Never the less, the child was smiling while looking up at Billy singing. She was the most beautiful child Sarah had ever seen.

Sarah looked up into Ben's misty eyes. "She's beautiful."

Billy was just finishing the song. Ben took Sarah by the hand. "I want you to meet her."

Ben led Sarah up on stage and over to his granddaughter. "Sweetheart…this is Billy's little girl. Her name is Sarah."

She raised her big blue eyes to Sarah. "I like that name. My baby is named Sarah."

Sarah knelt down to her. "That is a pretty baby you have, just like her mommy. What is your name?"

"My name is Amanda. Are you going to sing us a song?"

Sarah gave Billy a glance and a warm smile. "I can try." Her eyes turned back to Amanda. "What song do you want to hear?"

"Jesus Loves the Little Children."

"Do you remember the words?" Billy asked.

"I'm not sure if I do. It's been a long time."

Billy smiled. "Would you sing it with me?"

Sarah opened her heart, reaching up and touching Billy's hand. "There's nothing I would like better."

Sarah and Billy sang to the children, both sharing equal compassion for the tiny smiling faces that surrounded them. The music and songs seemed to have healing powers, frozen in this moment in time. The songs seemed to temporarily sooth the aches and pains of the children. With every song, Sarah's heart began to soften toward Billy. This was the first time, since the secret was revealed to Sarah, that she actually felt as if Billy was her real father.

18

Late that same evening, Sarah made a call to her mother. Sarah hadn't had a chance to call her to let her know how the first show went. She didn't want to wake Mary in the wee hours of morning, after the show had ended, and Jessie swept her away the next morning while Mary was at church.

Mary answered on the first ring. "I was just about to call you."

"Hey, Mom, I didn't want to wake you last night and I've been gone all day today."

"Tell me, how did the show go?" Mary asked, her voice brimming with excitement.

"Unbelievable," Sarah stretched out the word. "Mom, I wish you could've been here."

"So, you weren't nervous a bit?"

"I had butterflies in my stomach to start with. But they all flew away as soon as the music began."

Mary sighed. "I bet they just loved you."

"I think they did, especially after my second song, and even more after the next. Then Jessie added fuel to the fire."

"Details, I need details."

Sarah laughed. "Okay...for my second song I sang "Concrete Angel.""

"Oh my, that's a good one."

"I knew I had nailed it when I noticed tears from the audience. After the song, they chanted for more. It was supposed to be Jessie's turn to sing, but he wanted to please the crowd."

"That's the right thing to do. Did you sing another?"

"Yes indeed I did, Mom. I sang "I Will Always Love You." But I sang it just the way Whitney Houston did."

"Now I wish I had of been there. I bet the crowd loved it."

"They really did, Mom…after I added a twist."

"A twist?"

"Yes. When I sang the last chorus, I turned to Jessie. I was singing I will always love you directly to him as I walked toward him. He picked up on it and joined me in the middle of the stage, standing face-to-face as I sang the last lines. Then we ended the song with a kiss."

"That must have been great."

"Oh, Mom," Sarah paused, "then it was Jessie's turn to sing. He changed his original choice, wanting to keep the audience enticed. Jessie took me by the hand in the center of the stage and sang "I Swear." When he ended the song, we went into a long kiss. The audience went ballistic."

"Sarah, I imagine they did."

"Mom, I have never felt anything like that before. Jessie and I are planning to add some duets in the next show. We have picked out two to practice this week."

"That sounds like a great idea. I wish I could be there."

"Mom, why don't you come to the next show? I would love to see you. We will be in Jackson, Mississippi."

Mary hesitated. "I would really love to. Do you think Billy would mind?"

"I know he wouldn't mind a bit. I've seen the way he acts around you. You did say you thought he had once fallen in love with you."

"Sarah…that was many moons ago. I think that ship has sailed."

✳✳✳

The next morning, Billy and Sarah were to have a late breakfast before heading out to Jackson. Jessie skipped breakfast to make some important business calls. When Sarah entered the restaurant, Billy was already at a table having coffee.

Billy greeted Sarah with a kiss on her cheek. "Good morning, Sugar, where's Jessie?"

Sarah took a seat. "He had to pass on breakfast. He's making some business calls this morning. He's a hard worker."

"He sure is. I don't know what I'd do without him."

Sarah took a cautious sip of her coffee. "You'll never have to worry about that. He thinks the world of you, like a father."

The waitress interrupted for their order. Afterwards, Billy turned to Sarah. "Jessie's like the son I never had…and now I have my long lost daughter."

Sarah sat with her eyes in her coffee, thoughts drifting through her mind like a cold winter storm. She was reminiscing about Billy's drunkenness the night before last, and how close she came to leaving.

"I'm glad you decided to stay," Billy said, as if he was reading her mind.

Sarah jerked her head in his direction. "Jessie told you."

"No," Billy said, staring into her shocked eyes. "I heard the two of you talking."

She turned back to her coffee, her eyes straight ahead, away from his. "I thought you were passed out."

"I was out alright, but not unconscious. I owe you an apology."

Sarah had a disgusted look on her face. "I didn't really want to start the day off like this…but since you have opened that can of worms—"

Billy cut her off. "I'm really sorry, Sugar. I'll try not to let it happen again."

Sarah turned to him. She could see the sincerity in his eyes, but was blinded by the scenes from the night before last, playing over and over in her mind. "Try? You may want to try, but I don't believe you can help yourself. Have you ever tried to quit drinking?"

"Believe it or not, I have. A few weeks ago, while you were finishing up school, I decided to clean up my act. The shaking got so bad the next day I had to have a drink to settle my nerves."

"That wasn't just your nerves. That was a natural withdrawal symptom. Billy, you need professional help."

They stopped talking while the waitress set their plates before them. After the waitress walked away, Billy began seasoning his fried eggs with salt and pepper. "I don't need any help from any doctors. Anyway, they say that the first step to recovery is admitting the problem. That is what I've done. I've taken the first step."

Sarah took a bite of her omelet and stared into Billy's determined face. She knew that any further discussion would lead to an argument, which wouldn't help his situation. She figured this short step, of his own, might suffice for the time being. This would be a constant battle for him, one she was determined to monitor from here on out.

"Mom is coming to the next show," Sarah said as she watched to see his reaction.

Billy's face lit up. "That's great...she couldn't have picked a better one."

"A better one? What makes this one so special?"

"He grinned to himself for a moment, then made gradual eye contact. "Aren't you and Jessie going to perform a couple of duets?"

"Yes," she dragged out the word, "but I get the feeling that's not the reason for that smile on your face."

Billy laughed. "I'm not as good at surprises as Jessie is. I had planned a surprise for you, and now that Mary is coming, it will be even better."

"I can only imagine what it is. I won't ask you anymore. I don't want to spoil your surprise."

"It's too late for that. Have you ever been horseback riding?"

Sarah pointed a finger at Billy. "Now you've done it. The answer is, no, and you will have to tell me now."

Billy smiled. "I doubt if Mary has ever ridden a horse either."

"Okay, Billy, what has horseback riding got to do with the next show?"

"The owner, who is a good friend of mine—"

"That doesn't surprise me," she blurted out.

"He owns a Guest Ranch or Dude Ranch, as it is sometimes called. That's where people go horseback riding and stay at the ranch, in cottages."

"Yes, I have heard of them. Does this mean we won't be staying in a motel?"

"That's right. The ranch is located on the Pearl River. It is beautiful down there. Sunday evening we will all go horseback riding."

"That sounds like fun. So, tell me about these cottages."

"They are small, one bedroom cottages. The meals are served at the main house. But each cottage does have running water and a bathroom. You won't have to use a Johnny House."

Sarah laughed. "Thank goodness for that. So how many cottages have you booked?"

"Two."

Sarah raised an eye. "Just two?"

Billy grinned, knowing well what she was thinking. "Don't worry. Each bedroom has two beds."

"Still," she said, giving him a serious eye. "Just to be on the safe side, I will stay with Mom in one while you and Jessie stay in the other."

Billy laughed. "If that will make you more comfortable. Now aren't you glad you didn't leave?"

Thoughts suddenly flooded Sarah's mind. She looked at Billy, as she reminisced about him singing to the sick children. "You didn't ask me why I chose to stay."

Billy finished chewing his mouthful, washing it down with a sip of coffee. "I figured Jessie persuaded you."

"No," she responded then paused. "You surprised me."

Billy turned to Sarah, giving her his undivided attention.

Sarah smiled. "I was literally blown away at the sight of you singing to those precious children."

Billy grinned, while digging his fork into his eggs. "What, Sugar? You didn't think I knew the words to "Puff the Magic Dragon?"

Sarah laughed. "That too, but I didn't think you had it in you…especially not from the same man the night before. Who is Billy McCray?"

"I'm not a complicated man. I had a hard childhood, and then as an adult I was deprived of my child for twenty-one years, if you know what I mean. Through it all I've lived by one set of rules, do what you love and love what you do. And no matter how rough the road is you're traveling, make sure to stop and smell the roses along the way."

Sarah wiped her mouth. "There's nothing wrong with that… as long as you don't get lost in the weeds along the way."

Billy smiled. "You are your mother's child. That sounds like something Mary would say."

"I think Mom has a good head on her shoulders."

"A very good head on her shoulders…Mary is a fine woman."

Sarah took the last bite of her omelet. "Let's talk about those weeds you've been tangled up in for years."

"Weeds?"

Sarah washed her remaining breakfast down with her coffee that was chilling. "Yes…your drinking problem. You've admitted to the problem, but you need to face the underlying cause of why it began. You say it was because you were deprived from your child. I don't believe that to be the whole truth."

Billy gave her a surprised eye. "You don't." He grinned. "Does the prosecutor have a theory?"

"The prosecution does. The root of your problem stems from the fact that you fell in love with my mother and couldn't have her...and you are still carrying a torch for her."

Guilt kept Billy from making eye contact. "And how did the prosecution come up with that conclusion?"

"One...you have never married. Two...you haven't had a long-term relationship since Mom. Three, and the most damaging evidence of all, I've seen the way you look at her."

Billy finally met her stare and smiled. "You have a very strong case against me. You're forcing a confession from me. Yes, Mary stole my heart years ago...and still holds it hostage. So, there you go. I've confessed, but no crime have I committed. Loving Mary is not a crime, even though my heart has spent a lifetime behind bars."

Both sat in silence a few minutes, neither knowing where to go with this fragile subject. Billy decided to change the subject to spare his own feelings. "Am I wrong? Or did you not have the time of your life on stage Saturday night."

"Was it that obvious?"

"Very much so...you will never experience that feeling in a court of law."

Sarah grinned. "Your point...or should I ask?"

"I'm just saying...although I'm sure you'll make a great lawyer someday. It can never give you the same feeling you felt on stage. You were born to perform...on stage, not in a court room."

Sarah remembered the promise Jessie had said that Billy made to him. "Didn't you promise to take Jessie to Nashville?"

"I did...and I'm still working on that. Do you want to go?"

Sarah smiled as she picked up her fork, holding it toward Billy. "You get Jessie and me a record deal…and I will gladly skip law school."

Billy took his fork and clanked it against hers. "Sugar, you got a deal."

They both laughed out loud.

19

Sarah picked up Mary on Saturday afternoon at the airport in Jackson, Mississippi. With only two hours before show time, they headed straight to the club. A table was reserved for Mary nearest the stage. Sarah sat with Mary while she had a bite to eat. Mary was thrilled to be there because she knew Sarah and Jessie would be performing their first duets tonight. What she didn't know was that Billy was planning a little serenading of his own.

Billy was the first to perform. He went straight for the heart with his rendition of "Lady" by Kenny Rodgers. Billy was clean-cut and clean-shaven for the show. He wore jeans, cowboy boots, and cowboy hat, all in matching black. He also had on a thin black-leather vest with a loose-fitting white shirt underneath that was open from the chest up. From the moment the song began, Billy's eyes were locked on Mary. The lyrics pouring from his lips were coming straight from his heart, as if proclaiming his love for her to the world. The song, let alone his performance, caught Mary off guard. Her eyes were frozen to his, while his tender words took her back in time, back to when she briefly shared the same passion, still obvious in his eyes.

Billy's performance took Sarah and Jessie by surprise. Sarah could see the effect his words were having on her mother. She turned to Jessie, who had picked up on it as well. They both raised their brows and turned back to watch the rest of Billy's show. By the end of the song, Billy had slowly made his way across stage, his eyes still locked; never wavering, like the love he's held inside for so many years. He slowly came down on one knee, pouring out his heart to her with the last line of the song. He smiled while holding out a hand to her. Mary rose and gave him her hand with a smile. Billy gently kissed the back of her hand, causing an explosion of cheers from the audience.

Mary took her seat, acting as if her act was all part of the show. Billy got up and walked to the back of the stage to make room for Sarah and Jessie's performance. Sarah stared hard at him as he walked by. Billy could feel the weight of her stare. He cut her an eye, and then a devilish grin to match.

Sarah had to dismiss Billy and turn her concentration back to her act. She and Jessie were about to perform their first duet. They chose a steamy one by Faith Hill and Tim McGraw, one that holds a spot on the all-time great list "Let's Make Love." The lights lowered, leaving the band in the shadows, so the focus would be on Sarah and Jessie. The stage filled with a low fog, hovering barely ankle deep. A lone spotlight shone down on Sarah at one end of the stage as the music began, while another shone down on Jessie at the other end of the stage. Sarah was radiant in her white dress, resembling an angel from above. Jessie was equally handsome in his black and white outfit matching Billy's earlier.

Sarah began singing the first part, her eyes locked to Jessie's as they each slowly moved toward each other. They met at center stage, locking fingers together on each hand, moving in dangerously close, just as Sarah began singing the first chorus. They stood close, Jessie feeling her breath, soaking up the words as they stared sensuously into each other's eyes. After her chorus, Jessie began singing his part. He ran a hand gently through her hair as he began to sing to her, caressing her cheek softly, their lips close enough to touch. Sarah closed her eyes as Jessie sang to her, feeling passion from his touch. She played the part for the audience well, because she wasn't faking a bit.

They both sang the chorus together while in each other's arms. At the end of the song they fell into a kiss, and then smiled at one another. The crowd went crazy. Sarah finally tore her eyes away from Jessie, sending them straight to her mother. Mary was standing, her hands over her mouth as tears streamed down her cheeks. Sarah gave Mary a smile as she and Jessie drifted into the background.

It was Billy's turn to sing again. He took out an old guitar, one he only uses for special occasions like when he sang to the children at the hospital. Billy carried his old guitar and a stool out to the front of the stage near Mary. He took a seat on the stool, giving Mary a warm loving smile. Billy had hand-picked another great song with lyrics expressing his true feelings for Mary. He began singing "I Can't Stop Loving You" an oldie but goodie by Don Gibson, one of Mary's all-time favorites.

Mary's eyes watered from the first line. She knew in her heart that the first lyrics were words straight from his heart, as if he was the song writer. Billy's eyes never wandered from Mary's. When he saw her reaching up to catch a tear, he knew he had touched her heart, triggering his own locked-up emotions.

With tears dancing on his cheeks, Billy finished off the song with, "I love you, Mary."

The house erupted once again with cheers. Billy sat on stage, his teary eyes frozen to Mary's. After a long moment, he broke away by thanking the audience. This first set ended with each one of them singing a solo. Jessie sang Josh Turner's "Just to Be Your Man." Sarah sang "Before He Cheats" by Carrie Underwood. Billy wrapped up the set with "Always on My Mind," another by the great Willie Nelson.

Sarah came out on her first break to check on Mary. Mary didn't notice Sarah walking up. She was in deep thought.

"Mom," Sarah said, breaking Mary's train of thought. "Are you okay?"

Mary quickly grabbed Sarah's hand. "Oh, Darling. I feel like I'm sitting at the Grand Ole Opry or at the CMA Awards. This is one great show."

Sarah stared deep into Mary's eyes. "Are you okay?"

"Why wouldn't I be?"

"I saw how you were moved by Billy's singing, or should I say serenading."

Sarah was right. Mary was deeply moved, stirring long forgotten feelings she once had for Billy. Mary didn't want Sarah to know. "What are you talking about?"

"Mom," Sarah said, stretching the word, "I saw tears in your eyes. And you gave him your hand."

Mary smiled, trying to mask her true feelings. "It was a very touching song. I went along for the sake of the show."

Sarah held her stare, trying to read her mother.

Mary dropped her eyes to take a sip of her drink. "Didn't you see my eyes watering after your duet?"

"Yes."

"That was wonderful. I can't wait for the next one."

Sarah glanced at her watch. "I had better get back. We are doing the next duet to open the second set." She leaned over and kissed Mary on her cheek. "I'm glad you're enjoying the show." Her eyes narrowed. "I'm still not sure about you and Billy."

Mary smiled. "I'm a big girl. I'll be alright. I love you, Sweetheart."

Sarah gave her a quick smile, and then rushed back stage. Ten minutes later the stage slowly lit up. Out walked Jessie alone. He began singing "When I Said I Do" a great duet by Clint Black and wife, Lisa Hartman. Jessie sang the first verses alone on stage. When the chorus began, Sarah stepped out toward him, both singing in perfect harmony as they joined at center stage, eyes and hearts locked. They stood face-to-face, singing sweet lyrics to one another. Jessie began singing the verse after the chorus. With one hand he spun her around, dancing with her on stage as he sang. They came together, close, Sarah joining Jessie in song, cheek-to-cheek. Together, in each other's arms, they sang the chorus. They finished the song with a tender kiss. As they turned back to the audience, the applause became deafening. Sarah's eyes fell upon her mother, who was again flooded with tears of joy.

20

Sunday was a perfect day for horseback riding. The temperature hovered in the low eighties, with a hint of a westward breeze. The Mississippi sky was clear blue, like the Gulf that kisses the most southern part of the state. The ranch where they stayed was called The Appaloosa Trail, its name derived from the only breed of horses raised on the ranch. Not only are Appaloosas one of the most beautiful breeds, with their unique colorful coat patterns, but their eager-to-please attitude and mild disposition make them a popular choice for riding.

Billy and Jessie rode up, each pulling an extra horse, to Sarah and Mary's cottage. They dismounted just as Sarah and Mary came out to meet them.

"Aren't they beautiful," Sarah said as she rubbed her horse on its neck.

Jessie leaned in, giving Sarah a kiss on her cheek. "Her name is Sarah."

Sarah rubbed her horse's nose. "Well, Sarah, we should get along just fine."

Mary walked up cautiously. "Are you sure this is safe?"

Billy patted the horse on its neck. "Of course it is, Sugar." He rubbed the horse's nose as he began talking to the horse, like it was a person. "Sugar, you take care of this little lady. She's special."

Mary smiled. "You call everything sugar, even the horse."

Billy gave Mary a serious look. "Her name is Sugar."

Mary laughed. "You're kidding."

"Her name really is Sugar. I'm not horsing around."

They all laughed out loud.

"The ride begins in thirty minutes," Jessie said as he checked the saddle straps. "That's gives you beginners a little time to practice."

Sarah put her foot in the stirrup and mounted the horse as if she was an expert. Mary was still a little reluctant. Billy helped her up on the horse.

"What if I fall off?" Mary asked, fear in her eyes.

Billy smiled. "Sugar, you're not going to fall off. We will only be walking the horses, not galloping."

Mary looked around herself at the saddle. "Where's the seat belt?"

Billy chuckled. "Just hold on to the reigns. Sugar will take care of you."

Billy took hold of the harness on the horse's head and began walking. Mary squealed at first movement. "Whoa, Sugar! Where are the brakes?"

They all laughed out loud.

The trail ride got underway as scheduled. Due to Sarah and Mary's inexperience, Billy kept his bunch to the rear of the line, behind three groups of families, with children, along for the trail ride. The guide led the group, all one horse behind the other, down a scenic path alongside the Pearl River. Billy was at the tail end, right behind a nervous Mary who was actually enjoying the scenery. Many wildflowers were still blooming, but what really caught Mary's eyes was the abundance of Daisies in full bloom, her favorite flower. She also loved the bright yellows of the Black-eyed Susans that were scattered in bunches along the tree line and on the bluffs. The forest was filled with towering pines and gigantic oaks. The late-blooming magnolia trees stood out amongst the rest, with their large white blooms that filled the air with a charming fragrance.

The guide then led the group across an old wooden bridge, which crossed the river at a narrow point. The trail went on, winding upward into the forest. Squirrels played within the path, scampering across just in front of the horses, as if playing a game of tag. The gentle giants didn't pay any mind to the little creatures at their feet, even though their hooves barely missed the most daring ones.

The guide suddenly held up a hand, stopping the train of horses. He silently pointed to a small clearing in the woods to his right. In that opening, about fifty steps away, a small fawn stood, staring curiously back at the group. He had big ears and a blanket of white spots on his back. The fawn kept twitching an ear at a bright yellow butterfly that was determined to land on it.

"Mom," Sarah whispered loudly. "Look, there's Bambi."

Mary smiled. "Isn't that a beautiful sight?"

After about a minute, the mother stepped out of a thicket and stood close to her baby. She watched for a moment, and then nudged the fawn to move on. The guide whistled and the line of horses began moving once more.

Mary looked back at Billy. "Are there bears here?"

"Of course there are bears here, Sugar."

Mary's eyes popped wide open. "Is that why the guide is carrying a handgun?"

Billy noticed the fear in her eyes. He also remembered how much she hated snakes. "Not really, Sugar. Very seldom you'll see a bear. The gun is for the snakes."

"Snakes!" Mary snapped back, her eyes darting along the ground around her.

Billy grinned. "Yes, mostly rattlesnakes and copperheads."

Sarah had been listening in on the conversation. She looked back at Billy, recognizing his mischievous grin. "Mom, he's just teasing you."

Mary's eyes narrowed, staring back at Billy. "Billy McCray!"

Billy and Jessie laughed out loud.

Mary jerked her head back in Jessie's direction. "So, Jessie, you think that's funny, huh?"

"Watch out, Jessie," Sarah said in a playful manner. "Mom's got her sights on you now."

Jessie shot his hands high into the air. "I surrender!"

They all laughed out loud.

The three hour trail ride crossed back over the river and back to the main house. The guide led the group back towards the stables. When they got near the cabins, Billy rode up beside Sarah. "Our ride isn't over yet. Follow me."

Sarah and Mary shared a confused expression, while Jessie looked at Sarah and grinned. Billy dismounted at his cabin and rushed inside.

Sarah turned to Jessie. "Alright, Jessie, what's going on?"

He smiled. "You will have to just wait and see."

Mary looked back towards the stable, where the other families were getting off their horses. "I thought the ride was over."

"It is for them," Jessie responded, just as Billy was strapping his guitar case to his saddle. "This is Billy's personal trail ride he makes every time we come to Jackson."

Billy hopped on his horse. "Okay, follow me."

Billy began leading them in a different direction. He slowly picked up his pace, gradually pulling away from the other three.

"Look at Billy," Sarah said. "He's as giddy as a child on Christmas morning."

Jessie chuckled. "That's a good way of putting it, because that's exactly what he is."

"Where is he taking us?" Mary asked.

"I'll let you see for yourselves. Just wait until you see his welcoming committee." Jessie noticed that Billy wasn't slowing down. "Hey cowboy! Don't forget we have two rookies back here!"

Billy looked back, a smile growing on his face. He turned his horse around and trotted back to them. "I'm sorry. Where's my manners."

"Where are you taking us?" Mary asked.

Billy was still wearing a smile. "Oh, just to see some friends of mine."

"Some friends," Sarah said. "I'm not surprised. You have friends everywhere we go. I bet you don't have an enemy in the world."

"Oh, he's got one," Mary quickly spoke up.

Sarah chuckled. "I don't believe it."

Billy rubbed the scar above his eye. "Mary's right, Sugar. I've got the scar to prove it."

"I've always wondered where that scar came from," Sarah remarked.

Jessie laughed. "I'd like to hear this story."

"Well," Mary said, stretching out the word. "Are you going to tell the story?"

"Sugar…it was a long time ago."

Mary smiled. "Well, let me tell you—"

"Here we go," Billy said, shaking his head.

"It was his senior year," Mary continued. "It was Homecoming. Billy had the hots for the Homecoming Queen, the quarterback's girlfriend. And Sarah, you know who this quarterback is."

"Who?"

"Your future boss, Jack McAllister."

"Jack?"

"Yes. He was very popular back in those days. He was the star quarterback."

Billy mumbled under his breath. "Star quarterback my—"

"Billy!" Mary cut him off. "You had your chance to tell the story. Now, where was I? Yes, it seems that while Jack was playing his heart out on the field, Billy and Susan were making out behind the bleachers."

Sarah's mouth dropped. "Jack's wife, Susan?"

"She is now."

Sarah turned to Billy. "So, it was Jack that put that scar over your eye."

Billy bristled up. "Now wait just a minute, Sugar. Let's get this part of the story straight. Jack McAllister didn't put a scratch on me. I had him on the ground, beating him senseless. Four of his big linemen buddies dragged me off of Jack. Then they all four began pounding on me. After I was down on the ground, they kicked me. I ended up with a broken nose and some broken ribs. This scar came from one of their cleats...not Jack McAllister."

The path that they were on came up to a highway. Billy carefully led the group across and they continued along the wide shoulder of the road. When they rounded the next bend, a large two-story house stood on top of the hill. A long gravel driveway led up the hill to the house. As soon as Billy turned into the driveway, six children, all girls between the ages of five to nine, began running full speed down the hill to greet him. They all wore bright-colored sun dresses. Billy's eyes brightened at the sight. He stopped and got off his horse. Just in front of his horse, he dropped on one knee, his arms opened wide.

Sarah smiled at the children running down the gravel road to Billy. She turned to Jessie. "Whose children?"

Jessie looked deep into her eyes. "They are orphans. A local minister and his wife run the orphanage."

Sarah became misty-eyed while watching the children running, piling into Billy's arms, knocking him backwards to the ground. Billy was laughing while the children giggled. One took his cowboy hat off and put it on her head. The hat swallowed her head. All that was sticking out from under the hat was a smile and blonde curls. Sarah turned to Mary, who was misty-eyed herself.

Billy got up, brushed off his jeans, and then put two of the girls on his saddle. Jessie and Sarah did the same. They began walking the horses up the driveway, with the children riding and talking a mile a minute. One of the children on Sarah's horse was about six years of age. She had bright blonde curls and eyes as blue as the sky above. She had on a yellow sun dress that accented her long blonde curls.

Sarah looked at her and smiled. "What is your name, Sweetheart?"

"I'm Holly. Who are you?"

"My name is Sarah. I'm Billy's daughter."

Holly's face brightened up. "Billy is your daddy!" She looked at Billy. "I wish Billy was my daddy." She turned her stare back to Sarah. "You must love him very much."

Holly caught Sarah by surprise, but her statement didn't give Sarah that uneasy feeling like she once had. Sarah looked up ahead at Billy, who was laughing and playing with the two little girls on his horse. Thoughts flooded her mind, of Billy singing to the children at the hospital. Without her realizing it, Sarah's love for Billy had slowly grown, due in part by the revealing of his true nature. In Sarah's eyes, Billy's kind heart and loving ways had risen above his affliction.

Sarah turned back to Holly and smiled. "Yes, I do love him."

The little girl in the saddle behind Holly looked over at Mary. "What's your name?"

"My name is Mary. I'm Sarah's mother."

Holly jerked her head in Mary's direction. "You're Billy's wife!"

Mary smiled at Holly, glancing past her at Sarah. Sarah was smiling wide. Billy overheard Holly's remark. He slowly turned his head around, locking eyes with Mary.

21

Billy led the little angels on horseback up the hill to the yard. A middle-aged couple, both wearing wide smiles, waited patiently. Billy gave the lady a gentle hug. He then turned to the gentleman. They gave each other a firm hug, like old friends, both patting the other on the back. Mary had gotten off her horse, with a little help from Jessie, and stood close to Sarah.

Billy took Sarah by the hand, pulling her in front of him. "This is my daughter, Sarah." He then took Mary by the hand, pulling her up beside Sarah. "And this is her mother, Mary."

"Sarah and Mary, this is Steven and Marissa Jacobs. Steven is the local pastor. They also run this home—" Billy stopped himself. He didn't want to say the word orphanage in front of the children. "A home for rare and beautiful little girls."

The little girls all giggled. Marissa hugged both Sarah and Mary, welcoming them to their home. Steven stared at Sarah for a moment, and then Mary, as if he knew them both. He gave each a quick hug, welcoming them, and then turned to Billy. "God does answer prayers."

Sarah heard his statement clearly. She then noticed them sharing a smile, her curiosity peaked. The Jacobs led everyone into the backyard that was surrounded by gigantic old oak trees. A long picnic table was covered with a bright red and white checkered tablecloth that waved in the gentle breeze. Nearby was a homemade barbecue grill made from red brick. There were a half-dozen folding chairs set up nearby in a grassy area. The children, filled with excitement, quickly flocked to the grassy spot. Two of the girls dragged one of the chairs close to where they all were seated in the grass.

Mr. Jacobs placed a hand on Billy's shoulder. "I'll start the charcoal while you set up."

"That sounds like a plan," Billy said as he set his guitar case on the picnic table and opened it up.

Sarah waited for Mr. and Mrs. Jacobs to make their way to the grill, Mary following to lend a hand. Sarah touched Billy on his arm. "What did Mr. Jacobs mean by his remark, God does answer prayers?"

"Steven and I have become close friends. As a friend and a pastor, I have talked to him in the past about my life."

"Meaning, you told him about me…and Mom."

Billy quickly became defensive. "It was in private. I never mentioned names—"

"It's okay," Sarah cut him off. "You don't have to defend yourself anymore. I'm getting more used to the idea. I was just curious."

Billy smiled. "Thanks, Sugar."

"How did you meet?"

"It was about five or six years ago. They had a group of children on a trail ride. I've been coming by every time I'm in Jackson… for the kids."

Sarah smiled. "What about the big kid?"

Billy grinned.

Jessie leaned in. "You got him again, Sugar."

They laughed out loud.

Just then, Holly ran up and grabbed Billy's hand. She looked up at him with her big blue eyes. "Come on, Billy. We're ready."

Holly pulled him by the hand to the chair amongst the little girls. The Jacobs, Mary, Sarah and Jessie took seats in the remaining chairs. Billy began singing to the children. His first song was "This Little Light of Mine." The children sang along with Billy, their happy little faces glowing.

While Billy and the girls were singing, Sarah took notice out of the corner of her eye, Mrs. Jacobs taking her husband's hand, locking fingers. She laid her head on her husband's shoulder as she watched, a tear gently rolling down her cheek. Sarah looked over at Mary, who had also noticed. They shared a smile, both misty-eyed.

Billy and the girls went on to sing "Michael, Row the Boat Ashore," "He's Got the Whole World in His Hands," "If You're Happy and You Know It" and "Oh, How I Love Jesus."

Holly reached up, touching Billy's knee. "Does Sarah know how to sing?"

Billy glanced over at Sarah and smiled. "Yes, she does, Sugar. She can sing better than me."

Holly and another little girl ran to Sarah, each grabbing a hand, pulling Sarah out of her chair. They dragged her to Billy's side, Sarah laughing all the way. Sarah took a seat on the grass, crossing her legs like the other girls.

"Will you sing a song...please?" Holly asked with puppy-dog eyes.

Sarah couldn't refuse. "Okay, but I will need all of you to help me with this one. I know it's not Christmas, but this is one of my favorites. I know all of you know the words and the hand signs. It is "Away in a Manger.""

Their eyes opened wide as they each shook their heads up and down in excitement. Sarah began singing "Away in a Manger," while Billy picked the tune on the guitar, each child singing along with Sarah while using their hands, symbolizing the lyrics. When the song ended, the excited children piled up on Sarah, just as they did Billy when he arrived. Sarah and Billy made eye contact, both sharing a smile, a moment they would both treasure always.

They all sat down at the long picnic table, feasting on burgers and hotdogs with the fixings. They all held hands while giving thanks. Billy sat with Mary and Sarah on each side of him, the Jacobs directly across the table.

Billy wiped his mouth. "I've been meaning to ask. Where's Mary Beth?"

"A nice couple from Memphis adopted her last month," Marissa answered, and then looked up at Steven. "We're happy for her, but we sure do miss her."

Mary looked at Billy. "Who's Mary Beth?"

"Sugar, you would have loved her," Billy replied, then looked at Marissa. "I would like to show Mary and Sarah your picture album."

She smiled. "Don't you mean your picture album? After all, it was your idea."

Marissa went into the house and came back with a picture album. She handed it to Billy. He opened it, sharing the pictures and memories with Sarah and Mary. The pictures were from the past five years since Billy began coming by and playing for the children. The album was filled with smiling faces, from the children and Billy as well. Billy pointed out each child, calling them by name, telling something unique about each and every child. Mary had wondered why Billy mentioned Mary Beth out of all the other children. When Billy pointed Mary Beth out, Mary instantly knew why. Mary Beth was the spitting image of Sarah at that age.

22

It was nearing dusk when Billy and the others returned to the ranch. The sun was slowly sinking over the horizon beyond the lazy river, covering the churning water with a blanket of shadows from the trees lined along the west bank. As the shadows darkened, a new moon appeared on the opposite horizon from the sinking sun. The moon peeked over the horizon as a bright orange fiery ball in the sky. By the time the sun had completely faded away, the moon had transformed into a bright white beacon of light in the sky.

It was customary at night on the ranch to sit around a campfire beneath the stars. Most of the time there would be one or two who would tell ghost stories, making the children squeal. Sometimes there would be those who told jokes, depending on the company. Whenever Billy McCray was there, it was always singing around the campfire.

Billy began picking tunes on his old guitar, drawing the guests and their children from the nearby cabins. Once everyone was assembled around the campfire, their smiling faces glowing from the fire, Billy began asking for song requests. It was rarely that Billy was stumped by a request. He was like a human database filled with tunes of many kinds. While they were all singing as a group, the children roasted marshmallows on the ends of long wooden twigs. The bright moon inched slowly up in the sky, illuminating the surroundings as if it were daylight. The evening was getting late, some with small children retired to their cabins.

Billy turned to Mary. "Hey, Sugar, how about a moonlit stroll to cap the night off?"

Mary smiled, her eyes sparkling in the moonlight. "That would be nice."

Billy rose to his feet, lending Mary a hand and pulling her up. He handed his old guitar to Jessie. They began walking, arm and arm, down the moonlit path towards the river. Jessie and Sarah silently watched them fade away down the path.

"Do you think they will be alright?" Jessie asked.

"I'm not sure."

Jessie looked Sarah in her eyes. "What do you mean?"

Her eyes drifted back to Billy and Mary, who were barely visible from the distance. "I know where Billy's heart lies." She paused. "I'm not sure about Mom. Billy might be setting himself up for a fall."

Billy and Mary strolled slowly down the lightened path. Billy looked over at Mary, moonbeams bathing her face. "I'm glad you came this weekend, Sugar. You made it special for Sarah and for me."

She squeezed his arm tighter. "You made it special for me too. The show last night was great. Today was even better with the children at the orphanage." She looked up at him as they walked slowly. "The children really love you."

He gazed down into her eyes. "I really love them, too."

Mary smiled. "I can see that. Sarah told me about the children in the hospital in Baton Rouge. You would have made a great father. Why didn't you ever marry and have children of your own?"

"I thought I was already a father."

"You know what I mean. You could've married and had a houseful of children to spend time with. I know you must have met many women while playing from town to town."

He cut her an eye while shaking his head back and forth. "Yes, I was a real playboy. I had a different woman every night."

Mary could tell by his voice that he was joking. "I'm serious, Billy."

He quickly stopped, facing her. "Oh, I am serious, Sugar. It was like living a dream. Women coming on to me in every town we played in. Then one day, a special lady caught me by surprise. Up until that day, I had never felt love before." He looked deep into her eyes. "It was wrong. I knew it. But I couldn't help the way I felt."

At that moment, Mary knew he was referring to that one weekend they shared. Her mind drifted uncontrollably back in time. She remembered how she went to Billy, sharing a passion she'd never felt before or since then. She became flushed by his touch, her heart racing as he moved as close as a whisper.

"Then we made love," he continued, his eyes glued to hers. "Our desires were equal," he said, pulling her closer. "I knew right then that I was holding the only woman I could ever love."

Equally drawn, they melted into a long sensuous kiss. The passion that Mary once felt for Billy, which had never been stirred since, suddenly rose from the depths of her soul. Just before Mary had completely surrendered to Billy, that same guilty feeling from the past hit her like a tidal wave.

Mary pulled away. "We can't!"

"What do you mean, we can't?"

Mary refrained from eye contact, controlling her true feelings. "I can't. I'm sorry. Now is not appropriate."

Billy stepped closer, forcing eye contact. "Appropriate? How is this not appropriate? You kissed me back. It felt the same way it did twenty-two years ago."

"I can't help it, Billy. John has been dead less than a year. I feel as if I'm still married."

"John," Billy said with anger in his voice. "Even from the grave I still can't free myself from his shadow."

Mary's eyes narrowed. "Don't spoil this great weekend with an attitude. I can't help the way I feel."

Billy met her stare. "I know how you really feel, Sugar. You're just denying it." He began moving closer. "You can't tell me you don't want this."

Mary backed away. "Billy, please. Don't make this harder than it already is. It's too soon. This is not convenient."

Mary turned and began walking away.

Billy ran in front of her, stopping her. "Convenient? Love is never convenient? Love is spontaneous. Love is uncontrollable. Love catches you by surprise, when you least expect it, knocking you for a loop. That's what love is." He placed a hand on each of her arms. "I love you, Mary. And I know you love me, too. You did for one short weekend, and I felt it again in our kiss."

Mary, misty-eyed, looked up into his eyes. "I just can't, Billy." Knowing that if she stared into his eyes for very long she would fall back into his arms, she shut her eyes and turned her head. "Billy, if you really love me, you'll turn me loose."

"If I really love you?" Billy said, watching a tear that had slipped out from one of Mary's eyes. It glistened in the moon light as it ran down her cheek. "Mary, I've always loved you. I will never stop loving you. But, regardless of my feelings, I've always respected your wishes."

Billy slowly released his hold on her.

"Thank you, Billy," Mary said as she turned and walked away hurriedly.

Billy's heart ached while watching Mary fade into the night. He couldn't help but wonder if she would ever share a life with him, or would he have to keep his love for Mary bottled up inside, a curse getting harder and harder to tolerate. His hands began to tremble. Billy reached inside his leather vest, pulling out the one thing that he has relied on in the past to ease his pain. He twisted off the cap to his flask, quickly turning it up.

Jessie and Sarah were snuggled up next to the dwindling campfire. They held each other under the moon and stars. Sarah noticed Mary by herself. She was walking at a fast pace, almost in a jog, heading straight for their cabin.

"That doesn't look good," Sarah said. "I had better go check on Mom."

Jessie helped Sarah to her feet, and then gave her a quick kiss. "I'll go check on Billy."

When Sarah entered the cabin, she found Mary crying on the bed. Sarah laid beside Mary quietly, holding her while she cried. After a few minutes, Mary's crying was beginning to cease.

"How is Billy?" Sarah asked.

Mary rolled over, facing her daughter. "I'm crying and you ask how Billy is. What do you think happened?"

"Evidently Billy must have made a move on you and you weren't feeling the same thing."

Mary wiped her eyes with a hand. "Was it that obvious?"

"Come on, Mom. He serenaded you all during the show last night."

"But that was just a show. You and Jessie did the same in your duets."

Sarah wiped a lost tear from Mary's cheek. "Of course we did. We're in love and we poured out our feelings for each other in those songs. Billy was pouring out his true feelings for you with his songs. You couldn't tell?"

Mary sat up on the bed. "I'll admit I was very moved, but I thought it was for the show."

"That show was all about how he feels for you, Mom. You're bound to know how he feels! What happened when the two of you went for a walk?"

"He kissed me," Mary replied, staring out into space as she replayed the kiss in her mind. She could still feel his lips on hers and how much it felt the same as it did twenty-two years before, back when they shared a passion-filled weekend together.

Sarah noticed Mary's stare. She placed a hand on Mary's arm, breaking her trance as Sarah pulled her around, facing her. "You didn't try to stop him, did you?"

"I didn't," Mary admitted. "All those old feelings I felt for Billy years ago came rushing back. I didn't want him to stop." She paused. "But suddenly I thought of John. It was just like it was way back then. Then, I felt guilty and pulled away."

"And Billy?"

Tears filled Mary's eyes. "He's hurt. I didn't mean to, but I know I have hurt him again."

Sarah wrapped her arms around Mary. "Billy will be alright. I'm sure he'll come to understand what you're feeling."

While Sarah held her mother, thoughts ran through her mind that she didn't want to share with her mother. Sarah was hoping that this setback wouldn't send Billy into a drinking binge. Since her talk with Billy, she hadn't smelled whiskey on his breath. She knew he was trying to control his drinking, and she was proud of his efforts thus far.

Jessie walked down the path towards the river. In the distance, he could see Billy leaning against a fence post. The moon was so bright Jessie could see the cigarette in Billy's mouth and smoke swirling around his head.

Jessie walked up close and leaned against the wooden railing near him. "Are you okay?"

Billy hesitated. "Of course I am. Why wouldn't I be?"

"Mary seemed upset when she came back alone."

Billy pulled out his old friend again. He turned up the flask, draining it dry.

"Women!" Billy blurted out, just as he returned the empty flask back into its hiding place. "Who can figure them out? I sure can't. I don't think God can even figure them out. That must be why he hesitated before he made them."

Jessie stared at Billy, trying to figure him out. He could see that Billy was a little tipsy, but he couldn't smell the whiskey. "What was in that flask?"

"My old friend, Grey Goose," Billy said just before taking his last drag. He dropped the butt to the ground, smashing it beneath his boot. "How much do you love Sarah?"

"With all my heart. I hope to marry her someday."

Billy turned to Jessie, the bright moon revealing his teary eyes. "Then take some advice from an old fool. Let her know how you feel. Don't take for granted she already knows. And do whatever you need to do to keep her, even if you have to leave this business. Hell…I think you ought to go ahead and marry her today. If it doesn't work out, it would be less painful now than it would be if you carried that love alone, all your life."

23

Mary left the next morning on the earliest available flight. She made her escape without another confrontation with Billy. In her mind, it was best that way. She didn't want to hurt him any more than she already had. It was also the only way to prevent her true feelings for Billy from escaping. John's death was still fresh on Mary's mind and heart. She wasn't completely denying her obvious love for Billy, but she hadn't had enough time to fully heal, so that her heart could move on without a trace of guilt.

In Billy's mind, Mary's leaving without saying good bye confirmed his darkest fears. He believed that Mary didn't love him as he did her. He questioned whether she had ever loved him, though her kiss still lingered on his lips, a passionate kiss of love, not lust. In the back of Billy's mind, he had always carried the hopes and dreams that someday he would be reunited with his daughter and the only woman he'd ever loved, Mary. With a great portion of his hopes and dreams destroyed, Billy had to grab hold of his growing relationship with Sarah, the only thing keeping him from sinking into deep depression.

The following weekend was in Birmingham, Alabama. The show went on as planned. Sarah and Jessie both kept a close eye on Billy and his drinking. Billy did a good job of masking his feelings, as well as his habit. By switching to vodka, he could have his drink without the obvious aroma. He kept his drinking to a minimum while in Sarah's presence. After the show, when Jessie and Sarah were to themselves and Billy was alone with his wounded heart, Billy tried drowning his pain in alcohol. He had bottles of vodka stashed away that Jessie knew nothing about. Billy had other band members supply him vodka in secret. He began drinking more than he did before Sarah came to the band.

The band continued their southern sweep in the month of June. The next stop was Atlanta, Georgia, Jessie's hometown. Jessie showed Sarah around the city while keeping a watchful eye out for his biological father. Thinking that Billy was over his setback with Mary, Jessie spent more time with Sarah, taking her to the zoo and to the aquarium. While they were spending more and more time together, Billy was drinking heavily. They checked on Billy every night before turning in, but he was clever. Billy faked being asleep.

The next two weekends were scheduled in the sunny state of South Carolina. The first stop was Jessie's favorite, Charleston. Each week, Sarah and Jessie added more duets. Billy's show was slowly being transformed into the Sarah and Jessie show. They added such duets as "It's Your Love" by Tim McGraw and Faith Hill, "Don't You Wanna Stay" by Jason Aldean and Kelly Clarkson, "Picture" by Kid Rock and Sheryl Crow and "Whiskey Lullaby" by Brad Paisley and Alison Krauss.

On Sunday, Jessie took Sarah on a historic tour of Charleston in a horse and carriage. He even went as far as taking her to the Old Charleston Walking Ghost Tour. That afternoon, during the hottest part of the day, Jessie took Sarah to the tranquil beach of Seabrook Island. The less commercialized beach reminded them both of Nags Head. The more time they spent together, the deeper in love they fell. The more time they spent away from Billy, the deeper Billy sank into alcoholism, like falling into quicksand without a lifeline to pull him to safety.

The next show was in Columbia, South Carolina. Sarah and Jessie added only one more duet this week. They worked hard getting it perfect, probably because it was by Sarah's favorite singer, Carrie Underwood. The song was "Remind Me" with Brad Paisley and Carrie Underwood. Their hard work every week was paying off. Every club owner was trying to book more shows because of the reactions from the crowds. The show calendar for next summer was quickly filling, with shows covering entire weekends. Jessie was using their popularity to the band's advantage, by increasing the revenue of each show.

The last show in June moved into North Carolina, to the big city of Charlotte. Billy and Sarah had become very close over the past couple months. Their relationship had blossomed and matured beyond both of their expectations. This was not enough to deter Billy's drinking. The closer the shows got to Raleigh, the more Billy thought about Mary. The only thing that eased Billy's pain was alcohol. The disease of alcoholism had taken control of Billy, even to the point that Sarah was noticing changes in his behavior, even though he disguised it well. Billy was quickly irritated by minor hitches. With the addition of more duets, the practice time with the band was more often and longer for each session. It became harder and harder for Billy to hide the disease, because the disease needed feeding, requiring more alcohol on a daily basis.

On Sunday, Jessie and Sarah decided to go to the local amusement park, Carowinds. They tried their best to get Billy to go, but he was complaining of being nauseous from the Chinese food the night before. They went without him, but Billy's suspicious behavior tugged at Sarah's thoughts all afternoon. Before heading in, they decided to have a nice steak dinner. Shortly after ordering, Sarah decided to call Billy to see if he wanted some take-out. The phone rang, and then went to voicemail. Sarah hung up, but sat in deep thought, as if miles away.

"What's wrong, Sweetheart?" Jessie asked.

Sarah slowly turned her eyes toward him. "Billy's not answering. Do you really think he's sick?"

Jessie shrugged. "We ate the same food. How do you feel?"

"I feel fine," Sarah drifted off in thought for a moment. "Have you noticed Billy acting strange lately?"

"In what way?"

"He gets frustrated easily. He goes out to smoke more often. When he comes back, he's his old self again. It's like he's drinking, but I can't smell it. He has cut back on his drinking right much. Maybe that's what has him on edge."

Jessie began thinking. "I wonder how much he is drinking."

"I've only seen him with two mixed drinks each evening."

Jessie got lost in thought, back to when Billy was draining his flask, shortly after Mary had walked away from him.

Sarah noticed his wayward stare. "Jessie…where're you at?"

He slowly turned, his eyes meeting hers. "In Jackson, Mississippi. Do you remember when I went to check on Billy after your mom went to her cabin?"

"Yes. You said that you could tell it bothered him, but he brushed it off."

"There was something else I failed to mention. It didn't seem important at the time, but it does now."

"What was it?"

"When I found Billy, he was smoking a cigarette. He had been drinking from a flask that he had hidden in his vest. I don't know how much was in it, but he killed it right before my eyes. I thought it was strange because I didn't smell whiskey. Normally the smell is strong enough to knock you down."

"I know it. I can't stand the smell of whiskey."

"I asked Billy what he was drinking. He said it was Grey Goose."

Sarah's eyes widened. "Vodka?"

"Yes…and vodka is virtually odorless."

"That sneaky little—"

"Let's not jump to conclusions," Jessie said, cutting her off. "I hope I'm wrong."

"It makes perfect sense, though. In that case, he could be drinking a lot more than we think."

A worried look covered Jessie's face. "Let's hope not. We need to watch him closer. We've been leaving him alone too much lately."

"You normally go to the liquor store for Billy. Have you been buying him vodka?"

"Never. He loves his Tennessee whiskey. If I'm not buying it, then one of the guys in the band must be supplying him. Let's not say a word to Billy. I'll check with the guys and we'll watch him close this week."

Sarah placed a hand on Jessie's arm. "We have that show in the park this week in Greensboro."

"That's right. It's the 4th of July."

She stared into his eyes. "Mom is coming."

Jessie lifted a brow. "Then we had better watch Billy real close."

24

Billy's band packed up and moved on to Greensboro, the place where it all began, twenty-two years before. This was the place where Billy once tasted the sweet nectar of love, only to be quickly denied. The fond memories of that weekend, which Billy had cherished for years, now haunted him day and night. Billy was having the same lost feelings he had back then, when Mary went back to John. Soon afterward, Billy's heart had to endure a different kind of pain. It was the pain of having a child that he could never share a life with. It was the combination of those two pains that drove Billy to drinking.

Having Sarah in his life now eased much of that pain, but it was too late to save Billy from the grasp of alcoholism. With the recent rejection from Mary, Billy was spiraling deeper than Jessie and Sarah had realized. Their eyes were opened a bit after a little investigation revealed the amount of vodka that Billy had been supplied with by several different band members. Each one kept it a secret, thinking that they were the only one doing a favor for Billy. The staggering amount was cause for desperate measures. Jessie and Sarah planned to go through with this July 4th show. Afterwards, they planned to face this disease head on. Sarah was going to discuss Billy's disease with Mary in private, in hopes that she would come aboard to help battle this demon that had taken control of Billy. Sarah thought that with Mary's nursing background, she would probably know of a reliable treatment center specializing in alcoholism.

The 4th of July show in Greensboro was an all-day concert held in Center City Park, with a fireworks show at 11 p.m.. A bluegrass band had the first time slot, from noon to 3 p.m.. The middle time slot went to a local rock band, from 4 p.m. to 7 p.m. Billy's band closed the show, performing from 8 p.m. to 11 p.m.

Mary drove in from nearby Raleigh, meeting Sarah at the mall at 2 p.m. They had a late lunch, where Sarah opened up to Mary about the seriousness of Billy's affliction. Mary knew of a reputable treatment center in Raleigh. She was close friends with the manager. They had once worked together in the local hospital, years ago before Mary gave up nursing to be home for Sarah. While talking, Sarah researched the treatment center with her iPhone, by way of the internet. Both agreed that this treatment center would be best suited for Billy's needs, mainly because it was near Mary, where she could check on him every day. Mary's love for Billy was evident in the way she quickly volunteered her services to help him fight this disease. Their plans were to monitor Billy closely, not telling him of their plans, then confronting him first thing the next morning about the treatment center.

Sarah and Mary spent a couple of hours in the mall before heading out to the park. It was after 6 p.m. when they met up with Billy and Jessie, greeting them with hugs. Jessie hadn't let Billy out of his sight all day. Jessie was well aware that Billy had his old friend tucked away in his vest, letting him out for a taste every so often. Several times, just before a drink, Jessie noticed Billy staring at his hands, and then clinching his fists. It was a hot July day, but Billy was sweating profusely, noticeably more than anyone else.

The second band was finishing up their act, giving Billy and his band one hour to set up. Jessie took control of setting up the show, with help from Sarah, leaving the task of watching Billy to

Mary. Billy was getting suspicious. Looking back throughout the day, Billy realized that he was never alone for a minute, causing him to sneak around more than usual to get a drink. Now, with Mary stalking him, it was practically impossible, except to go to the restroom. The more Billy thought about it, the more feelings of being trapped grew.

Sarah opened up the show by singing a Martina McBride powerhouse song "Independence Day." Her strong vocals rang throughout the park, drawing people young and old the see her performance. The crowd was filtering in when Sarah and Jessie sang a duet for the second song. They performed a hot number belonging to Country Music's sweethearts, Tim McGraw and Faith Hill, "It's Your Love." Their sensual presentation with each other sent the crowd wild.

Billy came behind them with his song choice "Give It Away," a top hit of George Strait's. The crowd loved it, but Billy didn't receive near the applause that Sarah and Jessie had gotten. In past shows, the lack of applause didn't faze Billy. His anxiety from the lack of alcohol, plus the trapped feelings caused Billy to get frustrated. He fought to keep his emotions inside, while he continued to play on.

Sarah sang the next song, one by her favorite singer. She chose "All-American Girl" by Carrie Underwood. Sarah walked the edge of stage while singing, pouring out her emotions, playing to the crowd. The echoes of cheers rang throughout the park. Before the audience could finish cheering, Sarah and Jessie fell right into another duet, "Don't You Wanna Stay" by Jason Aldean and Kelly Clarkson. A crowd of hundreds squeezed in close to the stage. Everyone within hearing distance was drawn to Sarah and Jessie's performance, even the people who came early just to see the fireworks.

The band was scheduled for one short break midway through the set. Billy sang the last song before break. He sang "He Stopped Loving Her Today" by the late, great George Jones. It was a definite crowd pleaser, and one that Billy nailed time after time. Unnoticeable to the crowd, Billy struggled with the lyrics. Sarah and Jessie picked up on it instantly. They tossed concerned eyes to one another, without making it obvious to the audience. As soon as Billy sang the last note, Jessie stepped forward, announcing their short break. He then turned toward where Billy was standing. Billy had left the stage.

Sarah walked up to Jessie. "Billy went toward the restroom."

"He probably needs a fix. I had better go and check on him."

When Jessie entered the restroom, he found Billy leaning over a sink, splashing water onto his face with cupped hands. As Jessie slowly approached, he looked upon the face of a stressed out man.

"Billy, are you okay?"

"I'll be fine!" Billy barked, and then slowly turned to Jessie, meeting him eye-to-eye. "All I need is a little breathing room."

Billy held his angry stare for a long moment, then snatched a paper towel from the dispenser and stomped out. This was the first time Jessie had seen fire in Billy's eyes, the same fire he witnessed in his father's eyes just before a rampage. Jessie slowly exited the restroom while wrestling with haunting memories from his past.

Sarah was standing near the entrance when Billy steamed by her. A minute later, she watched Jessie coming out wearing a pale face, accompanied by a distant gaze.

"Jessie, you look as if you've seen a ghost."

Jessie stood still, his eyes wandering until landing on Billy turning up a flask. "I think I just did." His eyes followed Billy into the shadows, backstage. "Make me a promise."

Sarah looked up into Jessie's distraught eyes. "Sure, Darling… what kind of promise?"

He lowered his eyes, meeting hers. "After this show, no matter what it takes, promise me we'll get Billy the help he needs…even if it breaks up the band."

Sarah took his hand. "Yes, I promise…whatever it takes."

Jessie's eyes filled with tears. "Billy is the closest thing to a real father I've ever had. I don't want to lose him."

The band went back to work on the second half of the set. Billy had just enough alcohol to settle his nerves. He sang three songs in this last set, all without a hitch. He sang "Always on My Mind" by Willie Nelson, "Hello Darlin'" by Conway Twitty, and "Good Hearted Woman" by Waylon Jennings. Jessie sang two songs by Blake Shelton, "Sure Be Cool If You Did" and "Mine Would Be You." Sarah sang two songs by Taylor Swift, "Teardrops on My Guitar" and "Love Story."

Jessie set up the show to finish out hot, just like it began. The final song was a duet. Sarah and Jessie performed "Let's Make Love." The audience loved the show, especially the sensual way Sarah and Jessie sang to each other. Mary loved it too, so well that she forgot she was supposed to be keeping an eye on Billy. Sarah and Jessie leaned into a kiss after the last lyric, causing the crowd to erupt in cheers. At the same moment, the sky lit up with fireworks. Sarah and Jessie finished their kiss and stood face-to-face, smiling into each other's eyes. They lifted their eyes, simultaneously, to the sky above as streams of fireworks danced over their heads.

"He's gone!"

They quickly lowered their eyes to Mary's frantic face before them. "Billy's gone! He just disappeared!"

25

Rockets shot high in the sky above the park, bursting into the night sky with a multitude of bright colors, which reflected off the faces below. Jessie hurried to the restroom in search of Billy. Sarah and Mary waited outside, their eyes canvassing the crowd for Billy's familiar cowboy hat.

Jessie came out shaking his head. "He's not here!"

"Where could he be?" Sarah said, and then turned to Mary. "Mom, when was the last time you laid eyes on Billy?"

"Just before your duet. I'm sorry. I was so wrapped up in your performance."

Jessie laid his hand on Mary's shoulder. "That's alright, Mary. Billy couldn't have more than five minutes on us. He's probably hiding in a corner around here somewhere so he can take a drink in peace. Let's split up and search. I'll let the band know what's going on. Maybe they saw Billy. Keep your cell phones handy. Let's make a circle and meet back here."

The three split up and began searching for Billy. Sarah and Mary slowly worked their way through the thick crowd. The fireworks display illuminated the entire surroundings, helping in their search. Minutes later, the fireworks show ended, leaving them in the dark. Flood lights popped on, giving them just enough light to see where they were walking. Sarah and Mary made it back to the restroom area, but Jessie was nowhere to be seen.

"Where's Jessie?" Mary asked.

Sarah stretched her neck, looking around for Jessie. "I don't know." She spotted Jessie jogging toward them. "Here he comes. I hope he knows where Billy is."

Jessie ran up, out of breath and a frightened look on his face. "We've got a big problem. The Cherokee is gone."

"That's not good. He's pretty well intoxicated," Sarah said, and then raised her eyes to meet Jessie's. "Where would you go if you were Billy?"

"To a bar."

"You read my mind."

"He has his own booze, though. He might just be somewhere alone, drinking. During the break earlier, when I found him in the restroom, he was angry. He made a remark about not having room enough to breathe."

Sarah paced while in thought. "Then he could be anywhere, even back at the motel." She turned to Mary. "Mom…why don't you go back to the motel, just in case he goes there."

"I want to help, not just go to the motel and worry."

"You would be helping, Mom. You can also call the local hospitals and the police department. Jessie and I will search the nearest bars."

"Okay, I can do that."

"Thanks, Mom," Sarah said as they hugged.

Sarah and Jessie began their search by checking the watering holes nearest the park. They began to get worried after the first three bars were a wash. Mary eased their minds by calling to let them know that Billy was not at a hospital or the police department.

Sarah glanced at her watch. "It's after one. Where could he have gone? I was so sure he would've been at one of the nearest bars."

"I would have bet on it," Jessie agreed.

"And I thought he was doing so well."

Jessie stopped for a red light. He turned his eyes toward Sarah. "He was. I know he slowed down a lot after you almost left."

"Then what in the world happened?"

The light turned green. "Mary."

Sarah silently stared at Jessie. He threw her a quick glance. Just then his phone rang. Jessie pulled the phone out of his shirt pocket and checked the caller ID. He gave a look to Sarah like he knew who it was.

"Hello, Mike."

"Mike who?" Sarah whispered.

Jessie put a hand over the phone. "The club," he whispered back.

"Yes, Mike. I will be there in about fifteen minutes. Please, don't let him leave. Get his keys if you can. Thanks, bye."

Jessie dropped the phone back into his shirt pocket. "He's at the club."

"Why didn't I think of that? He's gone back to where this all began."

"Mike sounded desperate. He said that he had never seen Billy like this."

"What, drunk?"

Jessie ran a light just turning red. "He's drunk alright. And he's looking for a fight."

Sarah's eyes popped. "Fight? Billy?"

"Yes. Mike said he has already stepped between Billy and one man."

"Billy's not one to start a fight. You even said that the alcohol mellows him out."

Jessie glanced at the speedometer. He was trying to hurry without getting a ticket. "That's true…for whiskey that is. He's been hitting the white liquor pretty hard lately. That could be affecting him differently."

Sarah stared straight ahead, deep in thought, her eyes glued to the windshield. "Maybe the alcoholism is turning Billy into Mr. Hyde."

Sarah and Jessie entered the club just when a fight was being broken up near the bar. Suspecting that Billy may be involved, they rushed to the scene. Three men were trying to hold back what seemed like the biggest man east of the Mississippi. Billy was stretched out on the floor amongst several broken-up chairs. Mike, the owner, was standing between the angry man and Billy's stretched out body. Sarah and Jessie went to Billy's aid.

Sarah knelt down to Billy's side, noticing his swelling red cheek and eye. "Billy, are you alright?"

Billy flopped around like a fish out of water. "Let me up," he said, slurring his words to where they were barely comprehendible. "He got in a lucky shot."

Sarah looked back, seeing fire in the beast's eyes. "I think you had better stay down." She turned to Jessie. "Don't let him up. I'll try to get us out of here alive."

Sarah rose, facing the enormous man. "My father has had too much to drink," she said in a soothing voice. "He apologizes for whatever he said or did. He wants to buy you a beer."

"I what?"

Sarah sent her right foot flying backwards, burying her heel into Billy's knee.

"Ow!" Billy said as he grabbed his knee.

Sarah's pretty face and sweet voice calmed the beast. He looked down into Sarah's captivating eyes. "I don't like beer."

Sarah held his stare. "What would you like to drink?"

The man rubbed his chin as he thought. "I would like a strawberry daiquiri."

Sarah was shocked at his choice. She fought to hold a straight face as she turned to the bartender. "How about a strawberry daiquiri for the big guy." Her face cracked as she held up a finger. "Let's make that a double."

The bartender grinned. "You want extra fruit with that?"

Sarah pointed at him, her face turning red. "You got it."

Jessie and Mike pulled Billy to his feet. "Mike, we'll pay for any damages."

"That's okay," Mike quickly responded. "Just get Billy out of here before he gets killed."

Sarah took the arm that Mike had and handed him a twenty-dollar bill. "That's for the drink. Thanks, Mike."

He took the twenty and laughed. "I got one on Billy now."

Sarah and Jessie helped Billy along, wobbling and limping at the same time.

"I would be able to walk if someone hadn't kicked me in the knee," Billy slurred.

"Shut up," Sarah said crisply.

"Why are you mad with me? It's not my fault. He was getting sweet on me."

Sarah chunked her elbow into his side. "Shut your mouth. I'm trying to get you out of here in one piece."

They took Billy out and tossed him in the back seat of Sarah's mustang. Jessie searched the parking lot for Billy's Cherokee.

A few minutes later, Jessie slid in on the passenger side. "It's not here."

Sarah threw him a surprised eye. "Not here? Are you sure?"

"Yep," Jessie replied while throwing his arm over the back of his seat. He shook Billy, who was sleeping it off. "Wake up, Billy!"

Billy forced himself up in the seat, moaning every inch of the way. "Yeah."

"Where's the Cherokee?"

Billy stared at Jessie through half-opened eyes. "It's wherever you parked it."

"Billy!" Sarah barked. "You drove it here. Where is it?"

Sarah's bark opened Billy's eyes, jarring his memory. "Oh. We're at the club. I left it near a dumpster on the next street over."

"Why did you park it there?" Sarah demanded. "Why did you come here?"

Billy lowered his eyes. "Sugar, you wouldn't understand."

"Oh, I understand, alright. I understand that you are an alcoholic…and I'm getting sick and tired of it."

Her words stung, causing Billy's eyes to water. "Please don't leave me, Sarah. I'll do better."

Sarah had no intentions of leaving Billy. Their relationship had blossomed despite his affliction. She wanted to help him, not leave him. Since he believed otherwise, Sarah thought she would use it to her advantage.

"I got a good mind to pack up and leave," She said in a firm tone. "All you've ever been is a drunk, and that's all you'll ever be."

Jessie looked over at Sarah, shocked at the hurtful words spilling from her lips, aimed directly at Billy. Sarah gave him a wink without Billy seeing it.

Billy broke down and began to cry. "I can't lose you now, Sarah. I know I'm a drunk, Sugar. I need your help. Please help me."

His pleading was tugging at Sarah's heart. She had to turn her face to hide her watery eyes. When her eyes fell on Jessie, a tear was rolling down his cheek. She wiped her eyes and turned to Billy. "I want to help you, Billy. But you have to be willing to help yourself also. Together we can beat this. But only if you're willing to fight the fight of your life."

Billy looked up with childlike eyes. "I'll fight. I'll do whatever it takes to keep you in my life."

Sarah gave him a warm smile. "That is what I wanted to hear. We have found a treatment center for you."

Billy shook his head. "No doctors. They'll just steal my money."

"That is so ridiculous. Anyway, your insurance will cover most of the cost."

Billy didn't say a word, but kept shaking his head slowly back and forth.

Sarah was angered. "Don't tell me no! You said that you would do anything."

"Sugar, I don't have insurance."

Sarah's mouth dropped. "You mean to tell me that a man your age doesn't have health insurance."

"I can't afford it."

Sarah shut her eyes and fell back in her seat. "I can't believe this." She remarked, and then looked over at Jessie. "Can you believe it?"

Jessie shrugged his shoulders. "I don't have insurance either!"

Sarah crossed her arms over the steering wheel and flopped her head down on her crossed arms, shaking her head. "Now what do we do?"

"Mary," Billy slurred.

After a long moment of silence, Billy repeated himself. "Mary."

Sarah turned slowly, meeting Billy's drunken stare. "Mary? What about, Mom?"

"Mary can help me. She's a nurse."

Sarah gave Billy a look, as if he was crazy, and then carried it to Jessie.

Jessie was in deep thought. "Actually, that's not a bad idea."

Sarah held his stare while pointing back at Billy. "He's got an excuse. He's drunk. What's your excuse for agreeing with his crazy idea?"

"It's not crazy. Just hear me out. Your mom is a nurse—"

"Was!"

"I'm sure she can still take vitals, administer medications and keep a close watch on a patient. That's mainly what she'll be doing. The detoxification period lasts two to seven days, depending on the severity. That will be the most critical time."

Sarah's face was filled with confusion. "What makes you the expert? Where are you coming up with these calculations?"

"I've done a great deal of research on the Internet. I know Mary could do this. The only problem is getting the medications he'll need. Billy will need some sedating medications and then, anti-anxiety drugs are required."

Sarah's expression turned from confusion to surprise. "You really have done some research."

"Yes I have, a while back. I figured I needed to learn about it because I thought that I was going to have to tackle this disease alone."

Sarah looked back just in time to see Billy sliding down into the seat, repeating Mary's name over and over as he drifted out.

Jessie was watching the same scene. "Maybe your mom's friend at the clinic can help with the medications." He paused, while their eyes were still fixed on Billy. "We have to help him, Sarah. I feel as if he's my father too."

Sarah took Jessie's hand and looked into his misty eyes. "We will, Jessie. I promise. I'd just feel better if he was in a treatment center."

"I agree, but we can't force him. It's not a prison. He'll just walk out when he feels like it. Then we might lose him forever."

"You're probably right."

"Do you think Mary will go along with this?"

"I think she will. I think, deep down, that she really loves Billy. Mom is great at handling situations when they are thrown in her lap."

"How are you planning to spring this on her?"

Sarah grinned. "I'm heading back to Raleigh tonight, with Billy. You go back to the motel and tell Mom that Billy has agreed to get help. Don't tell her that she is the help he is referring to. Tell her to get some rest tonight and I'll see her at home tomorrow."

26

It was nudging noon, and the temperature was blistering hot when Mary arrived home in Raleigh. Jessie had held back to keep the band together. Mary was under the assumption that Billy was ready to admit himself into a treatment center. When Mary opened the front door, the aroma of freshly cooked bacon smacked her right in the face, causing her mouth and taste buds to leap for joy. Mary couldn't resist a mouthwatering BLT, and Sarah knew it all too well.

Mary walked into the kitchen. "Something sure does smell good."

Sarah was setting a plate filled with crispy bacon on the bar. "How about a BLT?"

"Most definitely. I wasn't hungry, but that bacon just woke up my appetite," Mary replied as she walked up behind Billy, who was seated. She wrapped her arms around him from behind and kissed him on his cheek. "I'm so proud of you, Billy. You've finally decided to get the treatment you need."

Billy raised an eye to Sarah just as she was cutting him an eye. "Yes," he said, dragging out the word. "I know now that I can't fight this alone."

"That's right," Mary said as she seated herself next to Billy. "I'm going to help you, Billy. Sarah's going to help you too. And I have a friend, a doctor, who I worked with at the hospital. He now heads a first-class treatment center. They specialize in alcohol and drug rehabilitation. You will be in very capable hands."

Billy held his tongue while throwing Sarah a desperate eye.

Sarah set the BLT in front of Mary. "Mom...have you ever treated anyone for drug or alcohol abuse?"

Mary's eyes were glued to the delectable sandwich in front of her. "I never had any alcohol patients. But I had my share of drug addicts."

Sarah watched Mary sink her teeth into the sandwich. "What's the difference in treatment for alcoholism verses drug abuse?"

Mary wiped her mouth with a napkin. "Sweetheart...this bacon is cooked perfectly."

Sarah watched her take another bite. "Thanks, Mom. What's the difference between the treatments?"

Mary raised her eyes in thought. "Mostly just the medications. Detoxifying drug addicts takes a lot longer than alcohol. Then there are the hallucinations that are much worse with druggies. Like I said, I don't know much about treating alcoholics, but it has to be much easier than for drug abuse."

Mary noticed Billy and Sarah staring at each other. She threw her eyes back and forth between the two. "Is there something I'm missing?" She then landed her eyes on Billy, who wore a guilty expression. "Billy...don't tell me you're having second thoughts."

Billy met her stare. "Well, Mary—"

Mary cut him short. "Don't well Mary me! Billy, you're so close. Don't turn back now." She took his hand. "Would it help if I stayed with you every minute?"

Billy cracked a smile. "Yes, it would, Sugar."

She squeezed his hand. "I promise I'll stay by your side the whole time. Sarah will stay too. Won't you, Sarah?"

"I promise, too," Sarah responded while moving in closer to Mary, preparing to drop the bomb on her unsuspecting mother.

"There you go, Billy. We will be constantly by your side, fighting this with you. What more can you ask for?"

Sarah decided to rescue Billy. "Mom, Billy's not backing out." She paused. "But there's a small problem."

"What's the problem?"

"Billy's agreed to get detoxed, but only if you do it."

Mary dropped Billy's hand, her face flushed with shock. "What!"

"Mom, please hear us out."

"Us? You mean to tell me you agree with this crazy idea." Mary rose to her feet. "So, you brought Billy here trying to trap me, and the BLT was just bait."

"Hear me out, Mom. We don't have a choice."

"We do have a choice. There's a treatment center a few miles from here."

"Mom, Billy doesn't have any health insurance." Sarah watched Mary's face turn pale as she dropped back down in her seat. "That's why we have to do it."

Mary turned to Sarah. "This is not like treating a cold or the flu."

"I know, Mom. But we have to try. It's the only way," Sarah pleaded as she took a seat by Mary.

Mary slowly turned her stare back on Billy. As they gazed into each other's eyes, flashbacks from years gone by flooded her mind. She pictured the way he was before alcohol took control of his life, back to when they consummated their love. Not only did Mary remember Billy's gentle and caring ways, but also the warmth of his touch. Her flashbacks quickly jumped forward in time, to the trail ride in Jackson. Mary pictured the girls running into Billy's outstretched arms. Then she remembered how he sang to the children, their smiling faces beaming with love for Billy.

Mary looked deeper into Billy's eyes. "Do you believe in me enough to do this?"

"Yes, Sugar…wholeheartedly."

"This is not going to be easy."

"I know, but it is something I have to do…for Sarah and for you."

"You should want to do this for yourself, for your own life."

Billy's eyes softened. "I do! You and Sarah are my life. I just want to return to the man I once was."

Mary gave him a warm smile. "That man is still in there, somewhere. I see parts of him peeking out every now and then. It's the alcohol that's keeping the whole man from emerging." She looked to Sarah, and then back into Billy's eyes, determination filling her eyes. "It's up to us three to bring out that man…to stay."

Mary finished her half-eaten sandwich, and then went into John's study for an important call. She dialed the number to her long-time friend, Mark Spielmann, who was the head of the nearby treatment center. After a long, in-depth conversation, Mary convinced her old friend to help her treat Billy in the comforts of her own home. In order to evade any legal repercussions, Dr. Spielmann had to examine the patient before prescribing any medications.

An hour later, the good doctor arrived at Mary's doorstep. Mary greeted him with a hug, his tall six-foot-five frame towering well above her head. Mary noticed two orderlies rolling a hospital bed up her sidewalk. "What is this?"

"I brought you some things you'll need."

Mary's eyes latched on to the restraint cuffs dangling from the railings. "Do you really think I'll be needing restraints?"

"Yes, Mary. I know you can remember how the drug addict's behaviors changed right before your eyes during withdrawal."

"Yes, but I didn't think it would be as bad with alcoholics."

"Not as severe, that's true, and for a much shorter period of time, minus most of the hallucinations. But still, there will be a critical two or three day span where you'll have to keep him strapped down."

Mary instructed the orderlies on where to place the bed. Her eyes followed them up the stairway as they carried the bed.

"When was the last time he had a drink?"

Mary glanced at the round-faced clock hanging on the wall. "Somewhere around sixteen hours now."

"Then he should be exhibiting some signs of withdrawal."

"He is. He's very edgy."

"Any trembling?"

"Just in his hands."

"Take me to the patient."

Mary took Mark into the kitchen, where Sarah and Billy sat at the bar having coffee. Billy stood and shook hands with Mark as Mary introduced him. Mark felt the moisture in Billy's hand, along with the slight quivering. Mary handed the doctor a piece of paper where she had recorded Billy's vitals from twenty minutes earlier.

He studied the paper, and then smiled at Mary. "You're still the proficient nurse you always were."

His eyes fell back to the paper. "Any known allergies?"

"None," Mary spit out. "I will be taking his vitals every half-hour."

"I brought you a vital signs monitor. It should make life easier."

Mary smiled up at him. "You're still the caring doctor you always were."

Mark grinned. He then turned and looked Billy directly in the eye. "Mr. McCray, I'm leaving you in the capable hands of Mary. But I want you to know that I'm a phone call away if you need me, day or night."

"Thank you, doctor."

Mary escorted Mark back to the front door.

He turned to Mary in the open doorway. "Mary, you're right. He's already showing signs of withdrawal." His hand slid into his front pants pocket, retrieving two bottles of pills. "The directions are clear. Any questions, just call me. I suggest by this time tomorrow, you use those restraints. You're in for a rough ride the next three days."

"Mark, what do I owe you?"

He smiled down at her. "Another hug ought to cover it."

Mary squeezed him tight. "Thanks, Mark."

27

By the end of the day, Mary had to begin sedating Billy. The combination of withdrawals from alcohol and nicotine was more than he could bear. Mary and Sarah took turns watching Billy. Though sedated, Billy wrestled with his dreams the whole night through. The next morning brought forth their first taste of battle. Billy was agitated at everything from the food to the lighting and even his new shiner. Sarah took the brunt of it, because Mary was resting from the long night before. Sarah handled him very calmly, but by lunch she was biting her lip.

Lunchtime brought Sarah some relief. Mary had awakened, feeling as if she could tackle most anything. That quickly changed when she first ran head on into Billy, which reminded her of Mark's suggestion of restraints by this time today. Luckily, it was time for his medication, and an increased dose at that. Once the dose kicked in, knocking him out, Mary secured him with the restraints. Mary decided to take advantage of this break by going to the kitchen for a bite to eat. Mary checked in on Billy at twenty-minute intervals, while she attempted some housekeeping that had gotten behind.

Mary was just heading back up the steps from the kitchen to check on Billy, when her doorbell rang. She stopped on the fourth step, waiting and hoping that whoever it was would leave. After the doorbell rang twice more, she decided she had better answer it before it awakened Sarah, or worse, Billy. She eased back down the steps and to the door. Without checking, she cracked open the door to see who was there.

Jack McAllister stood at the door. "Hello, Mary."

Mary slowly opened the door just enough to speak. "Hello, Jack. Is everything alright?"

"That's what I came to ask you. I haven't seen you in a while and thought I would stop by to check on you and Sarah."

Mary held him at the door. "We're doing fine. Sarah is fine too."

Jack wondered why Mary was acting strangely. "Mary...are you sure everything is okay?"

Before Mary could answer, Billy screamed at the top of his lungs. "Mary! Mary!"

Jack's eyes widened more with every scream. He pushed his way in. "What is going on here?"

"Jack! Don't!"

Before Mary could shut the door, Jack was half way up the stairs. When he topped the stairs, he caught a glimpse of Sarah darting into a door, the same door where the screams were coming from. Sarah ran to Billy's side, trying to calm him down.

Jack barreled into the room. "What the hell is going on?"

Sarah, wearing only underwear and a loose-fitting shirt of Jessie's, turned in surprise. "Jack?"

Mary rushed in. "Jack, you need to leave."

Jack's eyes darted around the room, Sarah's body blocking his view of who was in the hospital bed. "Not until you tell me what's going on."

"Jack McAllister," Billy spit out in spite.

Jack moved to one side to see who called his name. It was a familiar voice from his past. Anger filled his eyes when he recognized Billy's face, his thoughts drifting back to his high school days and the fight behind the bleachers after the homecoming game. "I don't believe it. It's Billy the kid, in the flesh." He spotted Billy's black eye. "Nice shiner you got there. I do recall one such as that, that you carried many years ago."

Billy grinned. "It was well worth it. Tell me…how is Susan doing these days? I can still taste her cherry chap stick."

Mary held Jack back. "Jack! Please leave!"

Jack held a scornful stare on Billy. "Mary, you shouldn't bring in stray animals. They are hard to get rid of once they get in."

"Jack, leave now," Mary insisted.

Billy's scar burned as he stared back into Jack's angry eyes. "What's the matter, Jack? Are you scared without your goons here to protect you?"

"Billy!" Sarah said, trying to calm him down.

Mary glanced at the vitals monitor, noticing Billy's blood pressure steadily rising. "Jack, please leave. Billy is very sick."

"He's sick alright. Sick as the dog he is. I can't believe you would allow such trash in your home, Mary."

Jack's words angered Sarah. Without thinking, she stepped up in his face. "Now you listen here, Jack. You don't talk to my father that way."

Her actions and words caught Jack by surprise. Jack took a step backwards. He looked at Sarah with confused eyes. "What are you talking about? We buried John in September. You—" He suddenly stopped, seeing that Sarah wasn't backing down. His eyes widened at the possibility of the truth. He looked at Mary. She wasn't denying Sarah's statement. "Don't tell me this is true. I bet John is rolling over in his grave right now."

"Jack, I think it's time for you to leave," Mary insisted.

Jack stared into Billy's eyes, and then looked at Sarah while shaking his head. "What a waste."

"What do you mean by that statement?" Mary firmly asked.

He looked back at Sarah. "The firm will no longer support Sarah's education."

Mary grabbed Jack's arm. "Jack, you can't do that. John set up—"

Jack jerked his arm loose, cutting her short. "John set up a college education for his daughter," he rolled his eyes toward Sarah, "not the illegitimate child of a scumbag."

"I've heard just about enough from you, Jack." Sarah said as she began loosening Billy's restraints.

Jack's eyes widened with fear, causing him to quickly turn and run down the stairs towards the front door. Mary went to Sarah, wrapping her in a hug. "I'm sorry, Honey. I wanted to stop you, but it came out so quickly."

"It doesn't matter, Mom. I never cared much for Jack anyway."

"But your education. How are you going to afford it?"

"I'm not worried about it. I can probably get a student loan. It's just three more years."

Billy began crying uncontrollably. Mary and Sarah turned to him.

"I'm sorry, Sugar. I didn't mean for this to happen."

Sarah took a washcloth and dried the tears from his face. "It is okay, Billy. It's not your fault."

"It must be the medication," Mary said, trying to figure out why Billy was so emotional.

"I'll pay for your college, Sugar."

Sarah wiped Billy's forehead while checking the monitor. "His vitals are coming back in line, but I think he's running a fever."

Mary placed her hand on his forehead. "I think you're right. I'll get the thermometer."

Billy kept crying. "It's all my fault. I'm sorry. I'll make it up to you, Sugar."

Mary stood by his side, holding a thermometer. "If you don't stop talking and put this in your mouth, I'm going to stick it in the other end."

Billy's eyes popped. He instantly stopped talking and held his mouth open for the thermometer.

Mary stuck the thermometer under Billy's tongue. "That's better. Now lie still." She waited. "I can sell this house."

"Mom! You're not selling this house!"

Billy began mumbling.

"Billy," Mary said as she stared into his bloodshot eyes. "If you mess this up, I will go in the other way." She looked at Sarah. "I don't need a house this big."

"Mom! I will not let you sell this house."

"What if I want to?" Mary asked as she pulled out the thermometer and read it. "It's a little high. That's normal. There's the beach house, too."

"Mom! No!"

Billy looked at Sarah. "I told you that I will pay for your college, I promise."

"Will you two stop it. I'll worry about this later." Sarah then remembered Billy's other promise. She looked into his eyes. "You just worry about that first promise you made to me. If you keep that one, I won't have to worry about college."

Mary wore a confused expression.

Sarah laughed. "Billy promised to take me and Jessie to Nashville. I told him I would forget about college if he got us a record deal."

Billy watched Mary and Sarah laugh. "I don't know why you two are laughing. I keep all my promises. You just wait and see."

28

The next night proved to be increasingly harder on Billy and Mary. She was glued to his side while he wrestled with the demon within. Sarah relieved Mary on scheduled intervals as planned. With every minute that passed, it became much more difficult for Mary to leave Billy's side. Her overflowing compassion had unlocked the sealed doors to her heart. When separated, Mary could not get any rest knowing the battle that Billy was going through in the adjacent room. Eventually, Mary never left his side, catnapping during the short periods of time when Billy would surrender to sleep.

Sarah accepted her role as guardian angel over Billy and Mary. She checked in constantly, day and night, on the inseparable pair. Just as the doctor had predicted, the fourth night brought out the beast. The prescribed medications were having little effect on easing Billy's torment. Mary didn't dare risk changing the dosage. Against her better judgment, she didn't call the doctor because Billy insisted she didn't. He couldn't bear her not being by his side for one single moment. Sarah joined Mary in this final battle, each holding on to Billy for dear life. Their combined love for Billy was the ammunition he needed to break free from the chains of this disease.

At 4 a.m., the disease suddenly released its hold on Billy, like a demon exiting a body after an exorcism. Mary's eyes rose to the monitor. Billy's vitals were slowly returning to normal.

"Is that the medicine kicking in?" asked Sarah.

Mary's eyes swelled. "No." She took Billy's hand, drawing it close to her face, a tear sliding down her cheek. "He has beaten it." Mary kissed his hand as more tears began to flow. "The worst is over now."

Sarah became misty eyed. "Mom! Are you serious?"

Mary smiled at Sarah, her cheeks drenched in tears. "Yes, Darling, Billy has done it. The detoxification period is over. That was the most dangerous time. That was the part that frightened me the most. He will still have to fight off the urges and cravings, but it should be all downhill from here."

"We have to make sure he never drinks again."

Mary looked back at Billy. "We shouldn't have to worry about that, now that you're in his life."

"And you, Mom."

Mary turned her stare back to Sarah.

Sarah rendered a smile. "You're still in love with him. I can see it in your eyes."

Mary thought for a moment, and then looked back at Billy. "I do love him. And for the first time, I can say it without feeling guilty." She turned to Sarah. "How does that make you feel?"

"I couldn't be happier, Mom."

"It's been less than a year since John died. Does this make me a bad person?"

"No, Mom. There may be some who would frown upon it because of the short period of time. And, I would probably agree, if Billy was a total stranger that had just come into your life. But you have a history with Billy. You fell in love with him years ago. Now, if you had told me that you were in love with Billy, the same day that you told me he was my real father…then I would've blown my top." Sarah looked into Billy's face. "But now that I've gotten to know the real Billy, like you, I can now admit that I love him. That is something I couldn't have said several months ago."

Mary reached across the bed, gently touching Sarah's arm. "That makes me very happy."

Sarah took her hand. "And, you loving Billy makes me very happy."

Mary could tell that Sarah was tired. "Why don't you get some rest now. He should sleep for a while."

Sarah left to take a nap. A few minutes later, Billy cracked an eye open.

"Hey, Sugar," Billy said in a raspy voice.

Mary smiled down at him. "How's my little soldier?"

"Tired…very tired," He replied in a weak voice.

"I know you are. You just rest now. The worst is over."

Billy looked at Mary through half-opened eyes. "You stayed with me."

Mary smiled. "Of course I did. I told you I would."

He took a deep breath. "Sarah stayed too."

"She certainly did. She loves you very much."

He struggled to smile. "I must be the luckiest man alive."

"Yes you are. Get some rest now. You deserve it."

Billy began drifting to sleep.

"I love you, Mary," he whispered.

Mary watched him drift off to sleep. She leaned over, gently brushing his lips with hers so not to wake him. "I love you, Billy," she whispered.

Mary watched him sleep for a few minutes while she kept a check on his vitals. Overcome by exhaustion, she crawled into bed by Billy, resting her head on his chest. She smiled while closing her eyes.

Sarah came in to check on Billy and Mary at 5 a.m. She took one step in the doorway and stopped. She smiled while watching Mary sleeping with her head resting on Billy's chest. Sarah eased back out of the room. A few minutes later she returned with a thin blanket. She carefully covered up Mary, pulling the blanket up close to her shoulder. Sarah left the room without disturbing the two.

✳✳✳

Billy opened his eyes at noon. Mary had gotten up and had taken a shower. She walked into the room just as he was stirring. "How are you feeling?"

He tried to speak, but then cleared his dry throat. "Tired and hungry."

She walked up close by his side and began loosening the restraints. "What would you like to eat?"

He looked down at his wrist. "Is it safe to do that, Sugar?"

"I think so, don't you?"

Billy rubbed his sore wrist. "Yes. I feel as if a weight has been lifted off of me." He watched her loosen his ankles. "I had a wonderful dream last night."

Mary looked up at him and smiled while loosening the last restraint. "You did? Tell me about it."

"I dreamed that I had two angels by my side last night." His eyes met hers. "Then after one had left, the other kissed me and said she loved me."

Mary grinned. "That was some dream you had. That angel that kissed you and said she loved you…do you think you'll ever see her again?"

Billy pulled Mary close. "I'm looking at her right now."

She threw her hand over his mouth, blocking his attempt to kiss her. "This angel says you need a shower."

Billy laughed as he eased out of bed. He grunted once his weight hit the floor. Mary watched him walk stiff-legged towards the shower. When he reached the corner of the dresser, he noticed his personal items that were in his pocket lying on the dresser. Among them was a half-full pack of cigarettes. Unaware he was being watched, Mary watched Billy reach down and slowly pick up the pack. He starred at the pack for a moment, then crushed them in his hand and tossed it in a nearby trash can. Mary smiled, and then headed towards the kitchen to prepare him some food.

After a long hot shower, Billy was drawn to the kitchen by the aroma of food cooking. Mary was busy stirring something in a pot on the stove.

Billy walked up behind her. "Now, where's that angel?"

Mary laid the spoon down and turned. This was the moment Billy had longed for a very long time. Billy took her in his arms and they kissed passionately. Sarah walked into the room clearing her throat.

Billy stood straight up while Mary buried her face in Billy's chest out of embarrassment.

"I forgot there was a child in the house," Billy announced.

"A child!" Sarah fired back. "This child has been babysitting you for the last few days! Now what have you got to say about that?"

Billy wrapped her up with a hug. "Thank you, Sugar. I couldn't have done it without you and Mary."

Sarah hugged him tight. "I'm glad to see you up. How are you feeling?"

"Like I've been run over by a truck. I might have to go back to bed after a bite to eat."

Sarah sat Billy down at the table.

Mary brought him a bowl of soup. "I know that soup is not a favorite during the summer, but it's best if you start off with something easy to digest."

Billy took a cautious sip. "Mmm, this tastes great." He cut an eye towards Sarah. "We need to have a talk."

Sarah raised an eye. "Sounds serious."

"It is. It's about school."

Sarah sighed. "Oh, that…I'm not worried about it right now."

"I am, and when I get my hands on that Jack McAllister—"

Mary smacked the top of Billy's head. "You're not putting your hands on anybody."

"It'll all work out," Sarah said while pouring Billy a glass of tea. "I'll take out a student loan. That's what the majority of the students have to do." She handed him the glass and took a seat beside him. "There might be one problem though."

Billy and Mary gave her their full attention.

"I will probably have to miss the first semester."

"Does that mean you won't start back until January?" Billy asked.

"That's right."

Billy's face lit up. "That'll work out just fine, Sugar. With the shows that you and Jessie have been putting on, there are plenty of owners begging for more. We can earn extra money just for your tuition."

29

Billy's major battle with detoxification had been won, but the aftereffects lingered on, leaving him very vulnerable. His next few days and nights was a struggle, but with the constant attention from Sarah and Mary, each passing hour became much easier. Sarah became Billy's guardian angel, strengthening their father-daughter relationship. Mary watched over Billy as well, unleashing the concealed love for him she had carried for many years. Their time together rekindled the passion they once shared many years before, making him even more determined to conquer all his demons.

After another week under the watchful eyes of Sarah and Mary, it was time for Billy and Sarah to rejoin Jessie and the band. Finally free from the bondage of alcohol and nicotine, Billy had a new lease on life, something to stay focused on, rather than drowning his sorrows away in booze. The daughter Billy had once watched from a distance was now a major part of his life. Mary was the final link of the puzzle, making Billy's life complete. She was the only woman he had ever fallen in love with. The resentment Billy carried for years toward his brother, John, stemmed from the fact that John had Billy's world in his possession, his only child and his only love.

Mary remained in Raleigh, agreeing to join them at chosen venues. She needed to stay in Raleigh to take care of some business. Mary planned to talk to Michael Morrison, the third partner in the firm. Mary hoped that she could persuade him to continue funding Sarah's education and fulfill the agreement that John had set into place, having Sarah fill his shoes as an equal partner if he was not able. Mary knew very well that Michael was a yes man, going right along with whatever Jack had always wanted to do in the past. Nevertheless, she was going to give it a valiant effort, though the odds were stacked against her.

Billy and Sarah met up with the band in Chattanooga, Tennessee, none too soon for Jessie. They arrived the day before the show, giving Jessie and Sarah time to reignite the fire in their duets, as well as their relationship. Late that evening, after the sun had relinquished the sky to a billion bright, twinkling stars, Jessie took Sarah to the top of Lookout Mountain to witness the beauty of the city below filled with lights, underneath the star-lit heavens above. Billy came along with them, not because they felt they needed a constant eye on him, but because Jessie had missed Billy. In addition, Sarah's relationship with Billy had grown to the point where she wanted to spend as much time as possible with him, as if their days together were numbered.

Later, after Sarah and Jessie had turned in, Billy picked up the phone and called Mary. Mary had insisted that Billy call her every night before bedtime while they were apart. She knew that this time of the day would be the hardest for him, the time when he was alone. They talked for an hour, while Billy scribbled on a notepad, a nervous habit he never realized he had.

The three got up bright and early the next morning, at the break of dawn, something Billy never would have done if he was still drinking. Jessie wanted to get an early start, before the sweltering heat blanketed the city. Jessie wanted to show Billy and Sarah the sights in Chattanooga, or the Scenic City, as it is also known.

Billy stood out on the balcony of the motel room with a cup of coffee in hand. Looking out over the water, Billy's eyes were glued to the gorgeous sunrise over the water.

Sarah blew across the top of her cup of coffee as she stepped up by his side. "You haven't budged from this spot in the last twenty minutes. That cup of coffee has got to be cold by now."

Billy smiled, his eyes staring at the fiery sky. "Yes it is, Sugar. I didn't want to miss this."

She turned her stare towards the horizon. "It's beautiful." She turned her eyes back on him, astonishment painted on his face. "You're acting as if this is the first sunrise you've ever seen."

"I'm sure it's not, Sugar, but I can't remember the last time I've seen one," Billy said, then pulled his eyes away from the sunrise and into Sarah's eyes. "I've missed out on so much in life. I can't believe I let alcohol steal my life from me."

"You can't keep looking back. You have to go forward from here, cherishing every single day and eager to see what the next day brings."

Billy smiled into her eyes, and then gazed at the sunrise once again. "Can we do this again?"

Sarah slid her arm within his, holding him tight. "Tomorrow and every day after, if you wish. We can watch the sunrise from every city we perform in. Then you can choose which one is your favorite. If you can't make up your mind, then we'll watch them all over again...together."

After a morning filled with sightseeing, they all rested until time to warm up for the show. Billy hit the stage like in his younger days. He hit every note crisp and on key with perfect timing, with his voice and guitar as well. He was full of energy, like a child after eating candy. Before, when Jessie or Sarah was singing their songs, Billy would play while standing in one spot. Now, Billy constantly moved about on the stage, interacting with Jessie and Sarah as they performed. Sarah loved it, and the crowd did too. Jessie had a hard time making Billy stop for a break.

The Billy the Kid Band brought the house down. With Billy's new lively performance and Sarah and Jessie's duets, the audience got more than their money's worth. Sarah and Jessie sang the last song of the night, a duet. They performed "Let's Make Love." The crowd went wild with applause. They whistled and clapped nonstop while the band was exiting the stage. Billy stood for a while, looking back at the crowd. He gave Sarah a grin just before he ran back on stage with his guitar in hand for an encore. The audience suddenly went death-like quiet the moment Billy began to play. Billy sang "He Stopped Loving Her Today." by George Jones, his favorite song.

Billy was still wound up when they got back to the motel and Sarah and Jessie called it a night. Billy called Mary and talked her ear off. He told her everything that had happened in detail, from the sunrise to the encore he performed. Mary could barely keep her eyes open, but she didn't have the heart to stop him because she could hear the excitement in his voice. He went on and on about how much Sarah meant to him. During their lengthy conversation, just like the night before, Billy scribbled on a notepad while talking. He jotted down words, phrases and sentences as he talked, not taking any notice to what he was writing down.

After Billy finally hung up, he rose out of his chair to prepare for bed. When Billy reached for his glass of water, his eyes landed on the notepad that he had scribbled on. He stood for a long moment staring down at the pad. Billy picked up the notepad, bringing it up closer to his eyes. He stared at the words on the paper and began to hum. He quickly grabbed his pen and added more words while changing others. Billy continued humming while scratching out and rewriting sentences on the pad. He laid the pad down and picked up his old guitar. Billy hummed continuously as he strummed his guitar over and over in search of the right melody. Billy played on his guitar into the wee hours of morning.

30

The next show took Billy and the band two hours south of Chattanooga into the city of Huntsville, Alabama, right in the center of Dixie Alley, a stretch well-known for tornadoes. This was not one of Mary's chosen places to come to, but Billy had begged her to come because he had a surprise for her. It involved Sarah, but he insisted that she needed to be present. With very little persuading from Billy, Mary agreed to fly in since it seemed very important to him, and the fact that she was missing him and Sarah like crazy.

First, before she could fly out to Huntsville, Mary wanted to speak to Michael Morrison about Sarah. She knew that if she could sway Michael over to her side, rather than Jack's, the firm would have to follow through with John's plan of funding Sarah's education because of a two-thirds vote on the matter. She stopped by the firm while in route to the airport. Luckily she caught Michael alone in his office. She greeted him with a hug and went straight to the point.

"Michael, I know that Jack has told you about Sarah by now."

Michael, in his starched white shirt and navy blue tie, lowered himself into his chair behind his desk. "You're talking about the fact that Sarah isn't John's biological daughter."

"John didn't know. You know how John was. It wouldn't have mattered. He would've loved her just as much as he did, like she was his own."

"You're probably right."

"This doesn't change the type person Sarah is, or how she will perform as a lawyer."

"I agree. It doesn't."

"So, I think the firm should follow through with John's plan. After Sarah graduates, she can fill John's position as a partner."

Before Michael could respond, Jack ran in. "Mary, I'm glad you stopped by."

Mary looked up at Jack. "I was having a private conversation with Michael."

"That's the good thing about a partnership," Jack remarked as he stepped behind Michael's desk. "There are no secrets."

Jack pulled open the top drawer, retrieving a multi-page document and tossed it on the desk in front of Mary.

Mary's curious eyes fell on the document. "What is this?"

"We feel that it is in the best interest of the firm to compensate you for your share."

Mary glanced over the first page. "Shouldn't you have said…I feel?"

Mary threw Jack a pair of angry eyes, and then targeted Michael. "Michael?"

"Well, Mary," Michael dragged out, painfully. "I have to think about what's best for the firm."

Mary raised her eyes toward the ceiling. "Is there an echo in here?" She dropped her eyes back on Michael and shook the papers at him. "When were you going to show me this?"

Michael sat in silence, with a look of guilt covering his face.

Jack sensed anger in Mary's voice. "Mary…there's no need to get angry. We've offered you a handsome price. This is just business, that's all."

"Business!" Mary repeated, firmly. "I never knew you could be so shrewd, Jack."

Mary looked at them both. The longer she stared at them, the angrier she became, clouding her judgment. "Where do I sign?"

Jack turned to the last page for her. "Sign on the dotted line. Here, use my pen."

Jack handed Mary his pen, gold plated and very expensive. Mary snatched the pen out of his hand. Jack's eyes watched the pen as it dived to the dotted line. Just as the ink hit the paper, Mary stopped. She slowly lifted her eyes, meeting Jack's gleaming face. She then turned an eye toward Michael, his face still covered with guilt.

Mary rose out of the chair. "Wait one minute. Suddenly I don't trust either of you." She picked the document up off the desk. "I think I'll have Sarah take a look at this before I sign."

Jack's expression flattened. "I don't know how long that offer will stand."

Mary grinned. "Don't you mean…we? I thought this was a partnership. I'll let Sarah read this over and I'll get back to you." She threw a hand over her mouth. "Oops…I mean the two of you. I forgot this is a partnership." Mary dropped the pen into her purse. "And thanks for the pen."

✳✳✳

Mary arrived in Huntsville late that afternoon, a full day before the show. Sarah picked her up at the airport. They embraced like two old friends. Sarah grabbed Mary's large suitcase on wheels and began pulling it along as they talked.

"Mom, I'm glad to see you. I didn't know you had chosen Huntsville."

Mary carried a small brown leather shoulder bag. She remembered the surprise Billy had mentioned that involved Sarah. Mary didn't want to give the surprise away. "I was really missing you and Billy." She paused. "And there's an ulterior motive for my being here."

Sarah gave her a curious stare. "It must be important to come all this way."

Mary unzipped a pocket on her shoulder bag while walking. She pulled out a brown manila envelope. "It's very important. I have a document I want you to read over before I sign."

Sarah's curiosity was peaked. "Sign? What is it you're signing?"

"Jack and Michael want to buy my third of the firm."

Sarah stopped dead in her tracks. A man walking behind her had to swerve in order to avoid a collision.

"What brought this about? Was this your idea?"

"No, Sweetheart. I just went by the office to speak to Michael."

Sarah pointed to a nearby waiting area. "Let's park it over there. I want to read this agreement."

They both sat down where they were to themselves. Sarah impatiently opened the envelope. Her eyes ran down the first page. "This is a very generous offer." She pulled her eyes from the page, staring into her mother's eyes. "Is this what you really want?"

"It wasn't my plan to start with. I went to Michael to persuade him to follow through with John's wishes. Jack rushed in and threw this in my face."

Sarah turned the page, her eyes skimming through the words. "I'm glad you didn't sign this."

"I almost did. I thought you said it was a good offer."

Sarah flipped to the next page. "The amount of money is good, but it doesn't pay in a lump sum. It's broken up over the next twenty years." She turned to the last page. "And there are so many loopholes in here. The only guarantee is the first payment. You probably wouldn't ever see another penny of it."

Mary's face reddened with anger. "That's why Jack was so eager for me to sign."

Sarah placed the document back in the envelope. "I can't believe Michael was in on this."

"He sat there and didn't say a word. He had to have known. That's why he had a guilty look on his face." Mary shoved the document back in her bag. "That makes me mad. I wanted to use that money for your education."

"I can't let you do that, Mom. That's money you'll need for the rest of your life."

"I've got money, Sweetheart. John had a nice insurance policy and we had savings."

"No, Mom. I've already talked to the dean and explained my situation. There's not a problem. I'll apply for a loan like everyone else. I'm making money with the band that will go for school. I won't be going back in January, not physically anyway. I'm taking what online courses I can while I'm working with the band. By fall, I'll have just two years left and at least half of that should be paid for. I'll be fine."

31

The next morning Mary rolled over in bed, reaching for Billy. After coming up empty handed, she cracked her eyes open. Dawn was just breaking, leaving the room still too dark to see clearly. Mary leaned over and turned on a lamp. As she was stretching to reach the light, the aroma of fresh-brewed coffee danced about her nose. She eased out of bed, letting her nose lead the way toward the coffee pot. Mary caught movement out the corner of her eye. The sliding glass doors to the balcony were open. A gentle breeze stirred the thin white drapes. She made a detour toward the balcony, where she found Billy sipping on hot coffee while admiring the sun peeking over the horizon.

"Sarah told me about your new hobby, watching sunrises."

Billy greeted her with a smile while she slid one arm around his waist, leaning into him. "Good morning." Billy kissed Mary on her forehead. "The sunrise is beautiful this morning, though it doesn't hold a shine to you, Sugar."

"Aren't you the sweet-talker early this morning? Where's my coffee?"

He offered her his cup. "Here you go, Sugar."

Mary turned up her nose. "Sugar is right…and I like a little cream too. I don't know how you can drink it black."

Billy went in and fixed her a cup, just the way she wanted. Mary blew across the top, and then took a cautious sip. "Mmm… not bad. I forgot to ask you last night. What's this surprise?"

"If I told you, then it wouldn't be a surprise, now would it, Sugar?"

"You said it involved Sarah."

Billy's eyes were glued to the rising sun. "Actually, there are two surprises."

"Two?"

"Yes, Sugar…and you're going to love them both. I'm not telling you anything else. You'll have to wait for the show tonight."

Mary stepped in front of him and smiled. "I might have a surprise of my own."

Billy's eyes dropped to hers. He recognized the desire in her eyes. "Oh yeah. Do I have to wait until tonight for your surprise?"

Mary took his hand, placing it within her top onto her warm breast. "Nope…that's the surprise."

Billy pulled her close. "I love surprises…especially at sunrise."

✳✳✳

Billy kicked off the show with a popular Lynyrd Skynrd hit "Sweet Home Alabama," drawing the audience to their feet, filling them with love and pride for their home state. Sarah and Jessie kept the heat on with a duet; "It's Your Love" by Tim McGraw and Faith Hill. Billy came back with a very popular solo, "Hello Darlin" by Conway Twitty. Mary was seated at a table nearest the stage. She couldn't get over how much sharper Billy's voice was without the effects of alcohol. Then Billy surprised her with a song she hadn't heard in a while, a tender ballad that brought tears to her eyes. Billy sang "Butterfly Kisses" by Bob Carlisle.

The last song of the set was one of Billy's surprises for Mary. It was a duet with Sarah. Since Billy's battle with alcohol, and the rapid growth of his relationship with Sarah, he wanted to perform a duet with his daughter. After finding the perfect one for a father and daughter, they worked on it all week. Sarah and Billy sang "Get Ready, Get Set, Don't Go" by Miley Cyrus and Billy Ray Cyrus.

Mary's face lit up the moment she realized that Billy and Sarah were singing a song together. She could tell that they had practiced long on it. Billy and Sarah enacted with one another as if they were doing a music video. Mary could see in Billy's eyes that he was singing from the heart. The words to the song held a great deal of meaning for him. Billy was actually releasing his inner feelings about Sarah someday leaving the stage to perform on a different kind of stage, in a court of law. He had spent the most part of his life dreaming of a relationship with his daughter. Now that it had finally come true, Billy didn't want to let Sarah go to follow her dream, but he loved her too much to stand in the way.

As soon as the song ended, Billy and Sarah joined Mary at her table, while Jessie tended to business backstage with the band. Mary greeted them both with hugs, applause still echoing throughout the club.

Mary smiled at Billy. "That's one."

Billy's eyes widened from fear that Mary might spill the beans about a second surprise.

Billy's reaction made Sarah suspicious. "One what, Mom?"

"One of my favorites, now."

Billy grinned while shaking his head, knowing that she had him going for a minute. "I'm glad you liked it, Sugar. The next song's for you."

"I hope you're not expecting me to get up on stage and sing it with you."

"No, Sugar," Billy said as he snuggled closer to Mary, "but you'll know it's about you."

Sarah leaned across the table toward them. "Will the two of you please act your age. Don't forget there's a child at the table."

They all laughed out loud.

Billy and Sarah went back stage to prepare for the next set. Since the band was performing in Alabama, Billy wanted to add a couple of songs to their repertoire. They added two songs from the band Alabama. Billy opened up by singing "When We Make Love" by Alabama. His eyes were locked to Mary's from the very first note. By the look in his eyes, Mary knew that he was singing this song from his heart. While Billy was singing tenderly to Mary, she was reliving her surprise for him at sunrise this past morning, the passionate way he made love to her.

The crowd erupted in applause. Before the applause had ended, Jessie came out with another song by Alabama, pleasing the crowd even more, bringing in another round of applause. Jessie chose "Feels So Right." The band had to play the opening notes over and over until the applauding had silenced. Then Jessie sang the tender words directly to Sarah. Sarah, like her mother, began reminiscing.

After a few more songs, Billy had the last song to close out the set. The band was just about to begin, when Billy suddenly motioned for the band to stop. The band members, including Sarah and Jessie, began looking at each other curiously.

Billy stepped to center stage, giving Mary a smile. "I would like to sing the last song before we take a break. This is a new song," Billy said as he eased to the side of the stage, taking a stool in hand. "The band is not familiar with this one. I'll be doing a solo."

Billy sat the stool down in the center of the stage. He motioned for Sarah to come and sit.

"For those of you who don't already know, this precious little lady is my daughter, Sarah," Billy said as he placed another stool next to hers.

Sarah sat on the stool and looked over at Jessie. They both shrugged shoulders at one another, not knowing what was going on. This had not been part of the show.

Billy went back across the stage and opened his old guitar case. Sarah was surprised to see him bringing it on stage. This was his first guitar, one that he cherished. The only time Billy ever brought it out was for special occasions, like when he sang to the children at the hospital and to the children at the orphanage.

Billy smiled at Sarah, and then turned back to the audience. "In case you all are wondering why Sarah has a strange look on her face…it's because this wasn't part of the show. As a matter of fact, she has never heard this song before." He paused. "And neither have you."

Billy propped himself on the stool beside Sarah. He closed his eyes and strummed the guitar once. By the expression on his face, the sweet sound must have touched his soul. When he opened them, the lights reflected off his glassy eyes.

Billy looked into Sarah's eyes. "This is a song I wrote. I call it…Sarah's Song."

Sarah was stunned, her eyes now matching his.

Billy watched a tear gently rolling down Sarah's cheek as he began to sing.

"My sweet Sarah
Sweet Sarah of mine
It began as a secret in the night
Two lonely hearts falling in love
Proving that two wrongs can make a right
The promise that followed, steering your life
Making you the special person that you are
Was the cause of my heart's torment and strife
I loved you from your very first heart beat
And to the depths of my soul as time went by
Knowing very well that we may never properly meet
You captured my heart at very first sight
Keeping it securely hidden through all these years
Same for your mother, since that secret in the night

Sweet Sarah of mine
Precious daughter I love
With a voice so sweet
Like an angel above
Sweet Sarah of mine
The light of my life
Sweet, sweet Sarah of mine

Fate has now brought you into my life
At a time when I was hopelessly drowning
You and your mother saved my life
My love for you opened my eyes to the light
Though my battles have not all been won
The love you've shown will steer me right
The power of love for a daughter
From her father whose been tested with time
Forms an unbreakable bond come hell or high water
I give thanks to the mighty Lord above
For his mercy on this wretched soul
And for my sweet daughter that I dearly love

Sweet Sarah of mine
Precious daughter I love
With a voice so sweet
Like an angel above
Sweet Sarah of mine
Light of my life
Sweet, sweet Sarah of mine"

When Billy finished the song, Sarah slid off the stool and wrapped him in a hug. The applause was deafening.

Billy could feel Sarah's tears rolling down his neck. "I love you, Sarah."

Sarah pulled back, looking directly into his eyes. "I love you, too…Dad."

Tears flooded his eyes. He pulled her tight. "Oh, how I have longed to hear those words. I never thought I would hear you call me, Dad."

Sarah could feel Billy's tears running down her neck. She smiled and squeezed him tighter.

32

The next morning Billy stepped out of his second floor motel room, alone with a cup of coffee in hand. He eased to the railing, which faced the east, while sipping on the hot brew. Dawn was just breaking, wakening the birds. They chirped and fluttered all around Billy, preparing for the day ahead. Billy didn't see another soul, but his senses detected someone outside on the floor beneath him. Cigarette smoke drifted upward, reminding Billy of his old habit. He took another sip of coffee, forcing his old cravings away, while moving safely out of the smoke's path. Just as the blood-red sun was peeking over the horizon, the door behind Billy opened, very slowly.

A sleepy-eyed Sarah stumbled out of her room. "I thought you might be out here."

Billy gave her a one-armed hug. "Good morning, Sugar. It's a beautiful morning."

Sarah yawned. "I bet you say that every morning."

He smiled. "I do now."

The door to Billy's room opened. Out wobbled Mary, half asleep, her hair uncombed and sticking out in six different directions.

Sarah laughed while messing up Mary's hair even more. "Oh, Mom. I love your new hairdo."

Playfully, Mary ran a hand through Sarah's hair, tossing it about, too. "I love yours, too, Darling."

Billy laughed out loud. "I want to thank the two of you."

Sarah and Mary stopped their playing instantly, both looking back at Billy through confused eyes. Sarah pulled her mother close to her side, and then placed her cheek next to Mary's. "Why? Could it be because we're so beautiful first thing in the morning?"

"That, too, but I wanted to thank the two of you for giving me life."

Mary raised a finger, pointing up toward heaven. "I think there's someone else responsible for that."

Billy smiled. "You know what I mean, Sugar. Yes, I thank God for giving me life. I tried to lose it in the bottom of a bottle. I want to thank you two for saving me, for giving me my life back."

They both wrapped their arms around Billy in a big bear hug.

"You're welcome…Sugar," Mary and Sarah said in unison.

Mary peeled herself off of Billy. "I need to go inside and throw a comb in this head."

"You had better do more than that, Sugar," Billy remarked.

Mary stopped, looking back over her shoulder at him. "Excuse me!"

"That goes for both of you," Billy added.

Sarah took a step backwards, throwing her hands on her hips. "You've got only one chance to get out of this alive."

Billy smiled wide. "I've got a surprise for you this morning. You better wake up Jessie. Time's a wasting."

"What in the world could you have planned this early in the morning?" Mary asked.

"I want to do something I haven't done in about forty years."

Sarah and Mary watched Billy's face brighten with excitement.

"I want to ride a roller coaster."

Mary's eyes popped open wide. "You want to do what?"

"There's a theme park not far from here. We're going to have some fun today. There's a water park, too. So grab your bathing suits and let's go."

"Honey," Mary said, while pointing to the rising sun. "There's no need to hurry. It'll be hours before they open."

Billy glanced at the sunrise, then back into Mary's sleepy eyes. "Okay, Sugar." He paused. "I want to be the first one there."

Mary turned to Sarah. "He's become a child again."

They all laughed out loud.

Billy was one of the first to enter the theme park. Just like a kid again, Billy wanted to ride every ride, and he did. He went for the roller coaster first, his favorite as he remembered as a teen, the last time he had ridden one. Mary rode what rides she could without getting nauseous. Sarah filled in and rode with Billy on the rest. Jessie gladly gave up his seat to Billy, seeing the pleasure it brought him, riding alongside his beloved daughter, having the time of their lives. After the deep southern sun began baking everything in sight, they spent the afternoon on water rides or just lounging around in the cool water to beat the heat.

Late that afternoon, after a nice dinner, Billy was driving the foursome back to their motel. The sinking sun was glaring in his eyes, causing him to lower the sun visor. As the road turned, the brilliant sunset was off to his left. Without warning, Billy pulled into a vacant lot and parked.

Mary watched Billy open his door. "What are you doing? There's nothing here."

Billy stuck his head back inside the opened door. "Yes there is, Sugar. Get out and I'll show you."

The three got out of the Cherokee and went to Billy, who was leaned against the side panel, his eyes glued to the fiery sunset.

Mary stood beside him, leaning gently against his arm. "Is this what you wanted me to see?"

"Of course, it's the simple pleasures that turn into priceless treasures in life."

Sarah slid in on his other side. "Is this another new hobby of yours?"

Billy smiled. "Not just sunsets and sunrises. I'm trying to make up for all the lost time in my life. I'm not going to take life's simple pleasures and beauties for granted any more. So, if it was to suddenly begin to rain, I would sing while walking in it and splashing in the puddles."

Jessie cleared his throat. "And I'll be the one driving you to the crazy house."

They all laughed.

Billy's eyes drifted left, falling on a hillside cemetery. He stared in thought for a long while.

Mary noticed his distant stare. "What's on your mind?"

Billy slowly turned his sights back on the sun. "Do you prefer a traditional funeral or cremation?"

Mary chunked an elbow into his side. "What prompted you to ask such a question?"

"It's just a question, Sugar. I'm sure this question has crossed your mind."

"We are not having this conversation," Sarah said, firmly. "Since when have you been thinking about death?"

Billy met her stare. "I'd never thought about dying until I began living."

Sarah looked deep into his eyes. "And living is what you're going to keep on doing. Talking about death will just bring it on...so stop it, Billy."

"What happened to calling me, Dad?"

Sarah's eyes narrowed. "When you're acting crazy, you're Billy. When you act like you've got some sense, then you're Dad."

Billy looked over at Mary.

She smiled. "Don't look at me to save you. I'm backing her one-hundred percent."

Billy surrendered with a smile, returning his sights to the sinking sun. The top of the fiery-red sun was barely peeking through the wooded horizon, giving the appearance of a forest fire off in the distance. They loaded up and headed back to the motel. The remainder of the ride was silent. As soon as Billy parked the Cherokee at the motel, Sarah and Jessie got out quickly. Billy didn't make a move.

Mary opened her door, and then noticed Billy sitting in deep thought. "What's on your mind, Honey?"

Billy's eyes followed Sarah up the steps. "Promise me something, Sugar."

"That depends on what it is."

Billy gave Mary a serious look. "Don't put me in the cold, hard ground. I want to be cremated and my ashes spread outside in the beauty of nature, somewhere that I'll be happy."

Mary closed her door slowly. "Why does it matter? It's just flesh and bones. Your soul leaves your body at death."

"I know that. But my body is still part of me. I don't want any part of me put in a dark, lifeless hole. I want to be set free, like the way I'm feeling right now."

Mary looked deep into his eyes. "I agree with Sarah. I don't like you talking about death. You're going to be here by my side for a very long time."

A smile returned to his face. "There's nothing that would make me happier. The thought just ran through my mind when I noticed that graveyard on the hill, where we watched the sunset. It would make me happy knowing that my ashes will be spread among the living."

Mary took his hand, bringing it up to her lips and kissing it gently. "If it will ease your mind, then I promise."

33

Billy was soaking up life in all its natural forms, by taking in life's often-ignored riches, such as the glorious rising and setting of the sun, and also the scenic views of the mountains touching the clouds. Whenever the opportunity presented itself to witness one of life's treasures, like a rainbow after a summer shower, Billy took full advantage of it. His eyes, once blurred by the presence of alcohol, were crystal clear and quick to take notice of the obvious we so often overlook, or take for granted.

Billy participated in activities he hadn't since he was a teen, like the roller coaster ride at the theme park. He also went fishing and bowling, two more things he remembered he loved, but hadn't taken the time to do in the last forty years. In all that Billy did, he included Sarah and Mary. Billy even took the time to go out and see a movie on a big screen. He found an old drive-in that had been renovated, like the one he visited frequently when he was young. Billy began attending worship services with Mary. On Wednesday nights, in whatever town they were at, Billy took Mary to church.

These family outings, plus Mary's maturing love for Billy was making it harder for her to stay away. In the beginning, she had planned to join up with Billy and Sarah at a few chosen shows, amounting to once every three or four weeks. Instead, Mary was going home to Raleigh about once every three or four weeks. Mary went home only once during the next six weeks. That one time was to get some business in order, including the business of telling Jack McAllister where he could stick his offer. Sarah had come up with a counter offer for Jack and Michael to scratch their heads over.

By mid-September, the band had made their way back to Jackson, Mississippi, one of Billy's favorite stops. The band performed another unforgettable show at the club, thanks to Sarah's duets, including the special one with her father. Billy had the next day all planned out for Mary, Sarah, Jessie and himself. It began late morning with a horseback ride, topped off with a picnic lunch at the river. Afterwards, they were to ride on over to the orphanage to visit with the girls.

Billy picked out the perfect spot to take refuge from the southern heat. Mary and Sarah stretched out a red and white checkered table cloth on the ground beneath two huge magnolia trees. Billy and Jessie tied the horses in a shady spot nearby. The four sat on the ground, enjoying sandwiches and southern sweet tea. Mary sat close to Billy on one side of the table cloth, while Sarah sat close to Jessie on the other.

Billy stared out at the scenic view of the river. "It doesn't get any better than this."

Sarah joined his stare. "I agree. I could do this every day."

The sound of Jessie's phone broke their serene moment.

Jessie glanced at the caller ID. "This is the call I've been waiting for."

Jessie rose to his feet, while answering the call. He walked slowly toward where the horses were tied; the phone glued to his ear and his pocket planner in his other hand.

Sarah's eyes followed him. "Jessie sure is a dedicated manager."

"You can say that again, Sugar," Billy responded. "That's probably an extra gig to help with your college fund."

Jessie rushed back, grinning from ear to ear. He handed the planner to Sarah. "We've got it!"

Sarah's face lit up. "The State Fair!"

"That's right, Sugar," Jessie said, mocking Billy. "The State Fair in your hometown of Raleigh, the second week in October."

Billy and Mary's eyes met, both sharing the same thought. He turned to Sarah. "Can I see that, Sugar?"

Billy took the planner from Sarah's hand. He looked at the date, and then quickly handed the planner to Jessie. "We can't do that one."

Sarah's mouth flew open. "What? I've wanted to do a show in Raleigh. Why can't we?"

Billy looked into her eyes. "Check the date, Sugar."

"I saw the date. The State Fair is always the second week in October. We are free that night, so what's the problem?"

Billy held her stare for a moment. "John."

Sarah dropped her face into her hands. "I can't believe I forgot."

Jessie turned to Mary. "I'm so sorry, Mary. That date completely slipped my mind."

Mary rose to her feet. "That's alright, Jessie." She sat next to Sarah, placing a comforting arm around her shoulders. "Are you okay, Sweetheart?"

"How could I forget that date?"

Jessie reached for his phone. "I'll call back and cancel."

Mary laid a hand on Jessie's arm. "Hold on, Jessie. Let's talk about this first."

Sarah lifted her glassy eyes. "Mom, that was the day he died."

With her hand, Mary gently brushed hair out of Sarah's eyes. "Technically, yes. That was the day we let him go. But, you know as well as I, that John was gone well before then." She paused. "We can visit John's grave the day before. Then you can still do the show at the fair. That is, if you think you'll be able to." She looked at Billy. "Honey, what do you think?"

"I'm fine with that, Sugar. But, I'm leaving it up to you and Sarah."

Mary took Sarah's hand. "What do you say, Sweetheart?"

Sarah dried her eyes. "I think that'll be fine."

After a couple of hours relaxing in the shade, they packed up and rode over the hill to the orphanage. Billy and Mary rode side by side, with Sarah and Jessie following close behind. Nearing the driveway up to the house, Sarah looked up, noticing the little girls lined up along the fence at the corner of the yard, waiting for Billy's arrival. All that was noticeable were the little girl's heads peaking over the top of the wooden fence, resembling a line of birds perched on a light line.

Sarah pointed toward the house. "Mom, look at the fence at the corner of the yard."

Mary's eyes rose, spotting the heads lined up on the fence. "Isn't that precious?"

As soon as Billy made the turn up the driveway, the girls broke loose, like flushing a covey of birds. Steven and Marissa Jacobs were standing in the yard, smiling as they watched the downhill race. Mary looked over at Billy, a smile highlighting his face. Billy galloped ahead and came to an abrupt stop. He quickly dismounted and dropped to a knee, holding his arms wide open. The girls leaped into his outstretched arms, the momentum sending Billy backwards to the ground. He was covered with giggling children. Billy and Mary piled the girls on their horses and walked them up the rest of the way up the driveway. Mary looked over at Billy, seeing the happiness glowing on his face.

Billy noticed her stare. "What? You look as if you want to say something."

Mary smiled. "I've never seen you so happy. You should've had three or four."

Billy threw an eye toward Sarah. "I have them all bundled up in one."

Mary took his free hand. "I love you, Billy."

"I love you, too, Sugar."

They greeted Steven and Marissa with hugs. As soon as the hugs were finished, two of the little girls began pulling Billy by his hands to come and sing under the oak trees. Sarah smiled at the sight. As soon as they got Billy seated, they ran to Sarah and pulled her to Billy's side. Billy and Sarah took turns singing songs to the little girls. Some they all sang together. Mary's eyes were glued to Billy the whole time. She witnessed the obvious happiness in Billy's face. Mary knew deep down that this place was dear to his heart. She could tell without asking, that if he had a choice, he would never leave this place.

After the singing was over, Mary slid her hand into Billy's. "You've brought me here twice. Both times you've seemed happier than I've ever seen you in your whole life. It can't be because you've beaten alcoholism, because the first time was when you were still enslaved to the bottle."

Billy's eyes wandered amongst the little girls, and then to Steven and Marissa. He then looked up at the old oak trees. "You're right, Sugar. This is my happy place. If I had to pick one place in the world to spend the rest of my days, it would be here. This is where I'm the happiest." He grinned, while looking deep into her eyes. "Next to being in your arms."

34

The second week of October arrived on the heels of a cool autumn breeze. Jack Frost had been busy at work, transforming the once vibrant green scenery into a flamboyant array of bright colors. Billy and his band rolled into Raleigh for the State Fair. The day before their show, Billy, Mary, Sarah, and Jessie visited John's grave. Mary and Sarah carried fresh-cut flowers in their arms. In Mary's arms was a beautiful arrangement of Shasta Daisies, her favorite, and the same type that John had once planted for her. Billy and Jessie watched, while Mary and Sarah meticulously lay the flowers on John's headstone.

The four stood silently, Mary and Sarah's thoughts drifting back in time, remembering John for the great husband and father that he was. Then, for the first time since John's death, Billy's thoughts drifted back in time. Childhood memories flooded his mind, memories that had been buried beneath bitterness. Billy looked up in thought, the changing leaves catching his eye, reminding him of how he and John used to play in mountains of leaves in their backyard as children. Billy's eyes drifted across the cemetery, white tombstones prompting memories of snow, and how he and John would sleigh ride in a nearby open field. A passing car caught Billy's attention. It was red in color, bringing back memories of his first car, a fiery-red Mustang. He recalled taking his little brother, John, for rides through town for ice cream.

These thoughts flushed out bottled-up emotions Billy had been carrying for years. He became misty-eyed. Sarah took notice of Billy's glassy eyes. It caught her by surprise, since he didn't show an ounce of emotion during John's hospital stay, and then death.

Sarah touch Billy's arm. "Are you alright?"

Mary looked up at Billy, surprised by his display of emotion. "Sweetheart, where is this coming from?"

Billy wiped his eyes with the palms of his hands. "It just jumped on me, Sugar. I was remembering how we were as kids. I don't know why."

Mary smiled at Billy. "I know why." She paused. "Now that you're sober, you're finally getting past the resentment you've been carrying for so many years."

Billy turned his eyes back to the headstone, starring hard at John's name. "How could I have been so stupid? He was my brother. We didn't share the same blood, but he was still my brother."

Mary saw anger in Billy's eyes. "Don't beat yourself up about it, Sweetheart. I'm sure John understands, now."

"That still doesn't make it right, Sugar. He's my brother."

Mary noticed Billy's face suddenly light up, as if a good thought had just crossed his mind. "What is it now? I've seen that look in your eyes before."

Billy leaned down, kissing Mary softly on her lips. "It's a surprise, Sugar."

Mary smiled. "You and your surprises."

When they returned from the cemetery, Billy went straight to work. He surfed the Internet, in search of two songs that he wanted to incorporate into the show for the next day. After downloading the lyrics and the sheet music, Billy went to Jessie, making him promise to keep it a secret from Sarah and Mary.

***

It was show time at the State Fair. Sarah had spoken to many of her friends, letting them know about their show. She was excited to finally perform in front of her hometown. Mary was equally excited. She talked to all of her friends about the show. The stage was set for another unforgettable show by The Billy the Kid band. Mary hadn't forgotten what Billy had said about having a surprise for her. Little did she know, Billy had more than one surprise up his sleeve.

Sarah lit up the stage with her opening song, "Man I Feel Like a Woman" by Shania Twain. She pranced around the stage, singing and waving to all her friends. Sarah was already on her way to stealing the show. Billy didn't mind, because she was making him proud. Billy took a little bit of Sarah's limelight when he sang his first song, "He Stopped Loving Her Today." Billy sang straight from the heart, displaying true emotions with every lyric, making it his best performance, ever. The crowd showed their appreciation with a long-standing ovation.

Mary was sitting with a group of her friends. They marveled at Sarah's raw talent, especially after her first duet with Jessie, "Let's Make Love" by Tim McGraw and Faith Hill. Sarah and Jessie put on a show of erotic desire as they sang to one another, exciting the audience with every sensual touch.

Just before intermission, Billy walked to center stage, looking out over the crowd. "I would like to dedicate this next song to my brother, John McCray."

Several in the crowd that knew John, whistled and clapped their hands. Mary's eyes widened, surprised by his dedication. She turned and laid eyes on Sarah. The same expression was painted on Sarah's face.

Billy smiled into the audience where the applause came from. "Thank you. I lost my brother, John, one year ago today. Like with many families, there are obstacles that sometimes interfere with the important things in life, like the love of family. I didn't realize that until I visited John's grave yesterday. None of us can go back in time and erase our mistakes. Don't make the same mistake that I did. If there is a loved one in your family, or even a once close friend, that you aren't as close to as you once were," he paused, his eyes watering, "make amends before it's too late for anything except regrets."

Billy slowly turned, signaling for the band to begin. With tears in his eyes, Billy sang, "He Ain't Heavy, He's My Brother," a song for the ages by The Hollies. He poured out his true feelings for John as he sang the tender words. Tears streamed down Mary's cheeks, her heart touched by Billy's show of remorse toward John. Sarah was equally moved, tears filling her eyes. Upon completion of the song, Sarah ran to Billy and wrapped her arms around him. The audience clapped and whistled while Billy and Sarah were locked in each other's arms on stage.

After the break, Sarah and Jessie moved the audience once again with their rendition of, "Picture" by Kid Rock and Sheryl Crow. Billy performed the next song, "I Cross My Heart" a legendary hit by George Strait. Before the crowd could stop applauding, Sarah and Jessie hit them with another duet, "Highway Don't Care" by Tim McGraw and Taylor Swift.

Time was moving on, with just a few songs left to sing. It was Billy's turn to sing. He waited for the audience to finish their applause.

Billy smiled at Mary, and then turned to his audience. "This is a song that I have always loved. It is also one that I thought I would never attempt to sing. Because my life has changed so much for the better in the last several months, for which I do not deserve, I thought I would now sing this fitting song."

Billy cleared his throat. Tears once more filled Billy's eyes, as he sang with conviction, "Why Me, Lord" by Kris Kristofferson. The crowd became misty-eyed while watching Billy sing from his heart, words that we often ask for ourselves. Billy sang each word with true sincerity, melting Mary's heart into tears that spilled from her eyes. Sarah went over and clamped to Jessie's hand, as they watched Billy perform flawlessly.

When the song ended, the crowd erupted in applause. Billy was so moved, that he bowed to the audience. As soon as Billy straightened up, he winced, as if in pain. He slowly raised a hand to his nose. He held out his hand before his eyes, blood coating his fingertips.

Billy's eyes rose toward the audience, landing on Mary. "I love you!"

He turned, facing Sarah, starring deep into her eyes, his hollow stare sending shivers down her spine. "I love you, Sarah!"

Before Sarah could move an inch, Billy dropped to the stage.

35

Sarah watched her world go crashing to the floor before her feet. Nearby paramedics could not save Billy's life. According to the doctors, Billy was already gone when he hit the floor. A brain aneurysm was the culprit, hidden away and undetected, like a ticking time bomb. Billy breathed his last breath while performing on the stage that he loved, alongside his only child that he treasured, witnessed by the only woman he had ever adored.

Once again, in exactly a year's time, Sarah's world was crushed. Mary's world was crushed, as well as Jessie's. The three were forced to console one another. The pain that Sarah felt was much sharper and deeper than with the loss of John. The loss of something you have worked for is always harder than something that was given to you. Sarah had loved John from childbirth, never knowing any difference, automatically accepting the role of his daughter. With Billy, it was different. Their relationship grew over time, beginning with complete denial. Billy's loving and caring ways opened Sarah's eyes and heart, nurturing their relationship, molding it into much more, a strong and unbreakable bond.

Jessie was stunned. The man he had looked upon as a father was gone, in the blink of an eye. He had forgotten what that kind of pain felt like. The memory of his mother's passing had been buried deep beneath his father's rage. His bond with Billy, like Sarah's, was strong and everlasting. Death has a way of breaking the strongest of men, making them shed tears like a child. Jessie wanted to be strong for Sarah and Mary, but the pain was too overwhelming.

Once the affairs were in order at the hospital, Jessie went home with Mary and Sarah. Jessie and Sarah sat at the kitchen table while Mary prepared a pot of coffee. Mary joined Sarah and Jessie at the table. All was quiet, except for the gurgling sound of the coffee maker. The aroma of fresh-brewed coffee slowly filled the air.

Sarah took a tissue and wiped her runny nose. "What do we do now, Mom?"

"Well, Sweetheart, I guess you have some planning to do."

Sarah's eyes widened. "Why me?"

"You're his daughter, his only child."

"I don't know what he would've wanted. A funeral here is not good. He's practically a stranger around here."

Mary recalled a conversation with Billy. "I know what he wanted. And I have an idea that I believe will make him happy."

"What is it, Mom?"

Mary smiled at her thought. "Billy told me that he wanted to be cremated—"

"Cremated!" Sarah spit out, cutting her off. "I don't know, Mom. Are you sure about this?"

"Very sure," Mary responded, taking Sarah's hand. "He was pretty adamant about it. Billy said he wanted his ashes spread out amongst the living. He didn't want a traditional burial, where his body would be laid to rest in the cold, dark ground." She paused, turning an eye toward Jessie. "And I know the perfect place to spread his ashes…his favorite place on earth."

Jessie smiled, squeezing a tear out. "I think I know where you are speaking of, beneath the gigantic oak trees at the orphanage, where he enjoyed singing to his children."

Tears flooded Mary's eyes. She threw her hands to her face. Too choked up to speak, she nodded in agreement.

Sarah put a loving arm around Mary, tears streaming down her face. "That's a great idea. I'm sure Steven and Marissa will be pleased to do it." She looked up at Jessie. "We have some phone calls to make tomorrow. I want to invite every club owner that Billy played for. I'm sure most of them would want to attend."

The following day, Jessie went to work spreading the sad news of Billy's death. His first call was to Steven and Marissa Jacobs. Jessie could sense tears flowing on the other end of the line. He brought up Mary's suggestion of a memorial under the giant oak trees where Billy played for the children. It was his favorite place on earth, and the proper place to spread his ashes. Steven and Marissa welcomed the idea, setting the date for the following week, on Saturday. Jessie continued on his mission, informing all the club owners of Billy's passing and details of the service to be held. By no surprise, Jessie had an overwhelming response. The owner of the ranch where Billy rode horses, volunteered to house all that came for the service.

✳✳✳

October, in the Deep South, is a pleasant time of the year. Mild temperatures prevail where extreme heat and humidity once dwelled. It was a perfect clear day, not a cloud in the bright blue sky. Steven and Marissa went all out in preparation for this ceremony, with help from the ladies of their church. The ladies of the church had prepared a feast for after the 11 a.m. service. Marissa had taken some chosen photos from her album, priceless photos of Billy and the children. She had them blown up and placed on large sheets of plywood. They were placed as a background, surrounding Billy's memorial marker, the very spot where he performed for the children, Billy's favorite place on earth.

Chairs for fifty were lined in front of the memorial site. Mary, Sarah, and Jessie, along with the members of the band, filled the front row. The rest of the seats were quickly filled, leaving a handful of devoted friends left to stand. Steven stood behind a podium, behind a table where the urn with Billy's ashes sat. Steven began with a prayer and then proceeding to telling the story of how he and Billy first met. Fighting back tears with every word, Steven made reference to the photos displayed, of Billy and the children he so dearly loved.

Marissa had set up an audio performance that she had taped of Billy singing to the children. Little did Sarah know, it was the one when she first came to this place, when she and Billy were still bonding. The music played on, causing tears to fall like spring rain. There wasn't a dry eye there, including the six adorable little girls that Billy and Sarah sang to that day.

Keeping the service short and sweet, Steven quoted a short scripture, followed by a prayer. Sarah rose and walked slowly toward Steven. Steven picked up the urn and handed it to Sarah. Sarah went over and stood over the memorial marker, the place where Billy sang his heart out the children. She opened the top and slowly poured the ashes out. Though the air was calm, not a breeze stirring, the ashes swirled and danced their way to the ground, as if happy to be in this place.

After the ceremony, Mr. Benjamin Schumacher, owner of The Cajun Queen in Baton Rouge, Louisiana, approached Sarah and Jessie.

He hugged Sarah. "That was a beautiful service. Billy would approve, I'm sure."

"Thank you, Ben. I'm glad you made it."

"I wouldn't have missed it for the world," Ben said, then paused as he became misty-eyed. "I'll miss my old friend. The children at the hospital will miss him, too."

Ben turned to Jessie. "I see you have canceled the show for next month. Does this mean the band will be breaking up?"

Jessie looked into Sarah's eyes as he answered. "We haven't discussed any future plans. I just went ahead and canceled the shows scheduled for the next two months."

Ben turned to Sarah. "I would like to run a thought by you."

Sarah nodded. "Sure, go ahead."

"I posted on the club's website about Billy's passing. Since then, I've been bombarded with requests for a farewell show for Billy."

"Really?" Sarah responded.

"It's true. Billy's band was very popular at the club, the most requested. After you sung at the last show, they have been begging for more."

Jessie took Sarah's hand. "He's right. Ben's been trying to get us to play there on a regular basis."

Ben rubbed his hands together. "This is what I'm proposing. Have the show, a farewell show, on the same date. All the proceeds, and I mean all of them including what comes from the food and liquor that night, will be donated to the children's hospital in Billy's honor." He paused. "I'm paying for the band out of my pocket, and that will be double the usual pay."

Sarah's eyes widened. "That is a very generous offer."

Ben smiled. "It's never enough, not for someone like your father. I hope you'll agree to do it. It's a month from now. Hopefully you'll be strong enough to do this. And maybe this show will help you decide about what's best for the future."

Sarah turned to Jessie. "What do you think?"

"I think it's a wonderful idea," He took Sarah's hand. "I'm all for it if you think you'll be up to it. And like Ben said, it will give us time to decide whether to keep the band going or not."

Sarah looked up into Ben's big blue eyes. "I think Dad would want us to. So, the answer is yes. We'll put on a show that Baton Rouge will never forget."

36

Mary arrived at the Cajun Queen, where she was greeted with open arms by the owner, Ben Schumacher. They weaved their way through the thick crowd, to a reserved table nearest the stage. Mary's eyes were drawn instantly to a large flat-screen television mounted on the wall to one side of the stage. Ben had a Memorial Video Tribute of Billy playing. Mary couldn't pull her eyes away from the screen. There were old pictures dating back to when Billy first started the band. As Mary watched the old photos, memories flooded her mind, reliving the long, loving weekend they once shared together, igniting the lasting love they shared.

The pictures played on, many of Billy on stage and off. There were pictures of Billy riding horses, and Billy singing to children at the hospital and the orphanage.

Ben smiled; as he watched Mary's eyes gleam. "What do you think?"

Mary slid an arm inside his. "I love it. Where did you get these old photos?"

"When I came up with the idea, I contacted Jessie. Before I knew it, my mail box was overflowing with photos from different club owners. Jessie must have contacted everyone Billy came in contact with. There are also pictures from the ranch, the orphanage and the hospital where my granddaughter is."

A tear rolled softly down Mary's cheek. "I would love to have copies of these to make an album for Sarah."

Ben smiled down at Mary, her misty eyes still glued to the pictures. "I thought you would. They are all yours. Plus, I made an extra copy of this video, just for you and Sarah."

Mary wrapped her arms around Ben. "Thank you, Ben."

By the time the band was ready to begin, the club barely had standing room. The large dance floor was filled with tables and chairs, to accommodate the overflowing crowd. Jessie and Sarah walked hand-in-hand, into a thunderous applause, to the front center of the stage. They wore matching outfits, blue jeans, white silk shirts and black-leather vests. Jessie also wore a black cowboy hat, reminiscent of Billy's favorite hat he so often wore.

Sarah smiled at the crowd. "Thank you all. Thank you very much."

The audience quieted down. Sarah's eyes fell on the Video Tribute playing. The first photo that caught her eyes was of her and Billy singing to the children.

Sarah's eyes watered, as she turned back to her audience. "We want to thank all of you for coming tonight. We have put together a show to honor Billy McCray, my father."

Applause filled the room at the mention of Billy's name.

Jessie could tell that Sarah was already struggling with her emotions, so he stepped up. "I am thankful for many things that Billy has done for me over the years." He smiled at Sarah. "I'm most thankful for the love of my life which he created."

Sarah returned his smile.

"Tonight we want to honor this great man with some of his favorite songs. We also have some new songs we picked out just for this show. Some of these songs will be difficult for us to get through, so please bear with us. Our wounded hearts are still fresh."

Jessie and Sarah drifted back into place on stage. The band began to play. Jessie began singing a moving ballad by Garth

Brooks, "If Tomorrow Never Comes." From the first line, Mary's eyes began to water. Sarah had to reach deep down inside, finding an inner strength, to overcome her own emotions. She joined Jessie for the chorus, their voices blending in perfect harmony.

Sarah sang the next song, a touching song by Carrie Underwood, "Temporary Home." She walked out to the edge of the stage, singing this tender ballad to the crowd. During the first chorus, she looked down and smiled at her mother. Mary smiled back through tear-stained eyes. The audience erupted in cheers at the end of the song.

After a few more of Billy's favorite Conway Twitty and Kenny Rodgers' songs, Jessie walked out to the edge of the stage. "For those of you who didn't know, Billy loved life. And, he loved his family very much. During the last year of his life, he connected with his only child, Sarah. Billy also reunited with the love of his life, Mary, Sarah's mother. The love he had for these two helped him conquer his battle with alcoholism." Jessie smiled wide. "Billy then lived the last months of his life to its fullest, enjoying every day, as if it was his last. That is what we should all do, and it is the reason I chose this next song."

Jessie stepped back, as the band began to play. Jessie sang "Live Like You Were Dying" by Tim McGraw. He sang the first verse while he and Sarah walked slowly toward one another on stage. They met face to face, locking eyes as they sang the chorus together. Their voices never wavered, even through the overpowering applause from the crowd as they sang.

After a long-standing ovation, Sarah walked out to the edge of the stage. She smiled out to the audience. "Billy—," she corrected herself, "Dad really loved it when Jessie and I did duets." She smiled down into Mary's eyes. "Mom really loves them, too. This next song is a duet. This is a new one, and definitely a fitting one. I hope you all enjoy it."

Sarah went back and met Jessie at center stage, where they stood facing each other. The moment the band began to play, the crowd applauded once more. They sang "When I get Where I'm Going" by Brad Paisley, joined by Dolly Parton. Just like Dolly, Sarah joined Jessie on the chorus, their voices lifting up together. They embraced at the end of the song. During the applause, Jessie took Sarah's hand, raising it to his lips and kissing it gently. Sarah rendered a smile, slowly pulling away toward center stage. She stood alone in silence, Jessie blending in with the band.

Sarah waited for the crowd to silence. Then she slowly lifted her head, giving the band their cue to begin the music. Sarah walked slowly toward her audience, as she began to sing "I Will Always Love You" by Dolly Parton. There was barely a dry eye in the audience when Sarah lifted her voice in the chorus. She fought gallantly to hold back her own emotions. All through the song, the audience could tell Sarah was singing from her heart, evident by the lone tear rolling down her cheek. Jessie sang the next two songs, giving Sarah's heart a break.

The show didn't stop for a break. They had planned a non-stop, three-hour performance. The show was down to the last two songs.

Jessie walked to the edge of the stage and looked out over the crowd. "This will be the last song I will be singing." His eyes fell upon Mary. He began to smile. "I want to dedicate this one to, Mary. She was the only woman Billy ever loved."

Jessie sang "The Dance," another great by Garth Brooks. His eyes were constantly on Mary, as he sang the tender words. The lyrics touched Mary's heart, drawing out tears that ran freely down her cheeks. Jessie stepped off the stage, continuously singing to Mary. He finished the song by kissing Mary on her cheek. Jessie held Mary close, sitting down with her to hear the final song of the night, a special one from Sarah.

Sarah walked out to the edge of the stage. She smiled down at Jessie and Mary, while waiting for the audience to calm down. She looked up at the audience. "I have come to realize, that losing a parent is the most painful thing a child can have happen to them, no matter what age. When Ben invited us to come and perform this memorial show for Dad, I had an overwhelming desire to write a song in honor of him. With Jessie's help, we came up with this song. The title is called, "Tears of a Child." She lifted her eyes toward Heaven. "This one is for you, Dad."

When Sarah lowered her sights back to her audience, the band began to play. With misty-eyes, Sarah began to sing.

"As a stranger, you came into my life
Through pain and struggle, I began to see
Past the thick darkness and dim light
The loving heart of the man you could be
It began with the innocence of a sick child
The way you touched her down deep
Bringing forth the glow of her bright smile
Touching my heart and making me weep

The tears of a child are tenderly brushed
As fragile as clear glass
Very painful when touched
The tears of a child are never hard or rough
They are delicate and sensitive
Never harsh or tough
The tears of a child are sweet and innocent
Increasingly more agonizing with age
Especially tears of sorrow, from time unspent

Our journey together has come to an end
Much shorter than we all had planned
The price of a child's sorrowful tears
For what God had already planned
I'll search for you every day at sunrise
Hoping to see your smiling face

I'll be saddened when you're not there
Though I know you're in a better place

The tears of a child are tenderly brushed
As fragile as clear glass
Very painful when touched
The tears of a child are never hard or rough
They are delicate and sensitive
Never harsh or tough
The tears of a child are sweet and innocent
Increasingly more agonizing with age
Especially tears of sorrow, from time unspent

The love of a father runs deep and wide
Through hardship, battles and time
Same too from a daughter filled with pride
The tears of a child are tenderly brushed
As fragile as clear glass
Very painful when touched
Especially tears of sorrow, from time unspent
Tears of sorrow, from time unspent"

Sarah was still wiping tears as she descended from stage and into the arms of Jessie and Mary. They embraced, sharing tears for the man they each loved in their own way.

Ben walked up, shedding a few tears of his own. "That was a wonderful show. I know Billy is smiling down on us right now."

A couple approached from within the crowd. They appeared to be pushing fifty years of age, by the abundance of gray in their hair. They were overdressed from the way the rest of the audience were dressed. The man was tall and slender, wearing an expensive three-piece suit. The lady with him was petite, wearing a red evening gown. Both were red-eyed, the lady still wiping tears. The man pulled out several business cards as he closed in.

"Excuse me," the tall man said, handing Sarah and Jessie a business card each.

Sarah and Jessie glanced at the card and then looked at each other with surprised eyes. The card was from a popular record label in Nashville.

"My name is Jeremy Brockman," he continued. "This is my wife, Bernice."

Bernice's glassy eyes sparkled above her beautiful smile. "That was a wonderful show."

Sarah and Jessie were still in shock, but both managed to thank her graciously.

Mr. Brockman smiled wide. "Would the two of you like to go to Nashville?"

Sarah's mouth flew open. "Are you asking us to audition for you?"

He slowly shook his head. "That won't be necessary. You've just performed the best audition I've ever heard, not to mention seen. The two of you have something special. I have a list of songs that I have been holding for just the right act. I think the two of you can rock the charts with these songs. I want the two of you in Nashville Wednesday. There will be a contract waiting for your signatures. What do you say?"

Jessie turned to Sarah. "You know how I feel about this. What about your law school?"

Sarah rendered a smile. "We can't pass up this opportunity. I can always go back and finish school, if this doesn't work out."

Mr. Brockman laughed out loud. "You won't have to worry about going back to school, Sarah. I've been in this business for over twenty years. I can spot talent…trust me. You two are on your way to becoming the next Faith Hill and Tim McGraw of country music."

Sarah looked over at Mary to get her opinion. Mary's eyes were filled with tears of joy, giving Sarah the answer she was seeking. She gave her a smile, and then turned to Mr. Brockman. "We accept. Thank you very much."

Mr. Brockman shook both of their hands. "Don't thank me. Thank William. I know I sure do."

Sarah, Mary and Jessie all looked at each other, puzzled expressions on their faces.

Sarah turned her puzzled stare toward Mr. Brockman. "William?"

"Yes," Mr. Brockman replied, and then turned to his wife. "I don't remember William mentioning his last name...do you, Honey?"

Bernice shook her head. "I don't believe so. All I can remember was his spellbinding eyes."

"Yes." Mr. Brockman concurred. "It was the strangest thing. We were vacationing in New Orleans, when this man walked up to our table at a restaurant. I'm not sure how he knew me, but I was compelled by his eyes. He said his name was William, and he told me about Sarah and Jessie. William told me about the show tonight, and how I had to be here. I've brushed people off for far less. But as he was telling me, and I was staring into his mesmerizing eyes, I knew I had to come. It was like I was hypnotized. Now I'm thankful I came, and thankful William came to me." He raised his eyes to the picture of Billy, still portrayed on the large flat-screen. "I'm a little confused though." He pointed toward Billy's picture. "This Billy McCray that you're remembering...who is he, again?"

"He's my father," Sarah proudly replied. "He passed away a month ago."

Mr. Brockman's eyes were glued to Billy's picture. "I thought I heard you correctly. But he bears a striking resemblance to William."

Sarah, Jessie and Mary just looked at one another.

"You can thank William for me when you see him." Mr. Brockman said, as he smiled at Sarah and Jessie. "I have to be going now. I have a lot of work to do. I'm looking forward to working with you two. The next live performance on stage for you two...will be at the Grand Ole Opry."

Sarah, Jessie and Mary watched Mr. Brockman and his wife, Bernice, leave. They turned to each other, astonishment filled their faces.

"Can you believe this?" Sarah said.

Jessie wrapped Sarah in a hug. "I'm still numb."

Mary looked at the two future stars of country music. "I can believe it. I guess Billy kept his promise after all."

Both looked at her, their eyes questioning her statement.

Mary smiled. "Nashville...Billy promised to take both of you to Nashville, didn't he?"

"Mom!" Sarah said in shock. "You don't really believe in ghosts, do you?"

"I never have in the past. I've never had a reason to. But you have to admit, it's a little strange. William is Billy's birth name. And Mr. Brockman did compare William to Billy's picture."

"But, Mom!"

Mary smiled as she looked up into Sarah's bright face. "Whether a ghost or not, I believe deep down in my heart, that somehow Billy had a hand in this because he loved you so very much. And if there's one thing I've learned from knowing and loving Billy McCray...it's that you never underestimate the power of love."